STOLEN BY THE FAE KING

MATED TO THE FAE KING - BOOK ONE

BAILEY DARK

"She's beautiful. But she doesn't care for me. If anything, she hates me. I watch her as she fidgets under my gaze, biting her plump lips. Those lips. I can't decide if I should nibble on them or simply yell at her for frustrating me so thoroughly."

Almost a thousand years have passed since King Altair of the Fae kingdom Alnembra was cursed by Maaz, a Bloodbane witch. A beast by day and a Fae man by night, Altair is desperate to find the Key. Now, the curse has almost run its course, but not before he discovers the existence of a woman who could break the curse and save him and his people.

Verity Chastain lives a normal life in New York City. On her wedding day, a beast swoops down from the sky to carry her into a world of fantasy and magic. Disbelieving and stubborn, Verity struggles to accept her new reality.

She and Altair go head to head in this fantasy-fueled romance. Can she find a way to break his curse? Or will he die as the physical manifestation of his sadistic personality; a beast?

CHAPTER 1

ALTAIR

The purple hue of the dusky sky is fringed with orange. The sun is rising, though the daylight hasn't yet driven out the night. The stars are still visible, winking above the city and the palace. From the roofless tower, I can hear my people below. The sounds of the city echo towards me, reaching high into the sky. Music and laughter. Laughter that will soon fall silent forever.

I narrow my eyes, staring angrily towards the mountain range in the distance. I can almost see Maaz and her Bloodbane witches soaring over the mountain peaks on their deadwood brooms. But it's only a flock of birds.

I'm running out of time. The night is disappearing, and the days are passing too quickly. I relish the night. Every morning, as dawn approaches, I can't escape the memory of the day Maaz cursed me. Cursed me to become the beast she saw when I refused her. I close my eyes, envisioning the moment.

Maaz, dressed in the blood-red gown slinked into my throne room as if it were hers already. She had dragged her long, black fingernails across my throat and down my chest, grinning.

I will never forget that grin. Cursed, she had said. Cursed for a thousand years or until I find a Bloodbane witch to break the spell and bind herself to me willingly. Cursed to die, along with all of my people, at the end of the thousand years.

And time is running short.

My stomach twists as Maaz's cruel smirk flashes through my mind again. The wind caresses my cheek, and I open my eyes to stare down at my city once more. My coat snaps out behind me as the wind speed picks up. It's coming from the West, towards the mountains.

I scowl, probably a reminder from Maaz. A gloat. A boast. She thinks she's won already. Fury sweeps through me, sending my blood singing with blood lust. I swing my arm towards the flag pole beside me, where my banner proudly waves, and drive my fist through the wood. It splinters loudly, and the pole breaks in half. It clatters to the stone floor of the tower, the flag coiled beneath it.

I stare down at it, at the black hawk poised to strike on the background of red fabric. My crest. My boot falls over the hawk as I drive the heel of my boot onto the hawk, soiling the flag. It's a useless symbol, anyway. Behind me, I hear the soft sound of Navi clearing her throat.

"When did you get here?" I ask, kicking the flag away.

She stoops and collects it from the ground. Always the loyal and patriotic soldier. "When you destroyed a perfectly good flag pole with a single punch," she says soberly. She folds the flag and cradles it in her arms.

I scoff. "Just let it go, Navi. That flag won't mean anything soon."

"Quitting right before the end?" Navi asks, her green eyes flashing. "I expected more than that from our King."

"King," I echo softly. "A failure, you mean."

"Altair," she whispers, placing a thin hand on my shoulder. "There is hope yet."

I turn to her, twisting my shoulder out from under her touch.

She tucks her long hair behind one of her pointed ears as I stare coldly at her. "Don't feed me lies, Navi."

"Your Majesty, the scholars have identified the one who may be the key to ending the curse. We know where she is now." Navi's eyes glitter. "Let me retrieve her."

"They found her?" I ask as the sun's first rays slip over the horizon. Disbelief taints my voice. We've searched for her for hundreds of years, many of the scholars said it was impossible. That her existence was only a legend, a rumor.

I have waited almost five hundred years for this moment.

"I will go," Navi says.

"No." I turn to the rising sun. "I will."

CHAPTER 2

The lipstick is too red for my tastes, a sharp contrast to my ivory skin. I sigh and wipe at it with a towel, smearing it a little. Tara clucks her tongue at me and uses a finger to gentle nudge my face towards her. She takes the towel and adjusts the makeup.

"What's on your mind? I thought we decided on that lipstick yesterday," she says. "Let's go nude."

I puff out my cheeks as she rummages through her makeup bag for a more natural lip. "I wouldn't say that I'm getting cold feet . . . but I am apprehensive, let's say."

She paints my lips with the nude coral tone. Much better. "You don't have to do this, you know. You can back out now if you want to, run away even. I've got your back."

"Tara, you know I can't," I say. "My parents, well, they need this."

Tara purses her lips and steps back to survey the whole picture. "God, you look gorgeous. Come look." She maneuvers me in front of the floor-length mirror so I can see myself. "You're the prettiest bride in the world."

Dressed in a sleeveless ivory lace gown that hugs my figure

before falling loosely to the floor in twirls of tulle, I do look the picture of a bride. Even if I don't quite feel it. "The nude lip looks much better," I remark, twisting my head to the side to admire my hair.

Tara, my maid of honor and best friend, adjusts her purple gown and huffs. "Henry is such a manipulative bastard."

I know instantly what she's talking about. We've had this discussion many times since I first accepted Henry's proposal. "Hey." I eye her. "It's not unusual for a husband to help his in-laws financially."

My father ended up with expensive medical bills after his chemotherapy a few years ago. He and my mother pay them off little by little, but they won't have made a dent in the debt by the time they pass. And worrying about the debt falling on my shoulders has made them physically sick numerous times. We do what we can. Henry saw the struggle and promised to help if I married him.

"Yeah, but most men don't bribe women into marrying them with that," Tara says pointedly. "I mean, would you have married him if he hadn't led with that offer?"

I sigh. "No. I mean, I don't know. Maybe."

Tara snorts.

"Henry is a good man. He can be kind and affectionate. And he obviously knows how much I care about my parents, that's a good sign."

"He's also a bit of a dick most of the time," Tara says as she picks at her manicured nails.

"Okay, maybe more often than not," I mumble. "What are you doing? You're supposed to help me feel confident in my decision, not try to talk me out of it."

She grips my shoulders and stares intensely into my eyes. "What kind of a friend would I be if I didn't have your back? I just want you to be happy, are you going to be happy with Henry?"

"I . . ." I take a slow breath in, "I . . ."

She frowns, "Verity."

"I need some fresh air," I say, waving my hand in front of my face like a fan. In less than an hour, I'll be walking down the aisle towards Henry. I'll be binding my life to his for the foreseeable future. It's a lot.

A lot a lot.

Tara ushers me towards the door. "Go outside and get yourself together. I'll come get you in time for the ceremony, and if you change your mind just text me. I'll drive the getaway car."

I flash her a grateful smile as I hurry to the back door leading out of the manor. Henry picked the venue for the ceremony and reception; a beautiful villa on the hills of Connecticut. I peek out the door before I exit, checking to make sure no guests are lurking around, or Henry for that matter. But the way is clear. The villa is a sprawling house with several wings. I picked the most secluded one to keep my big reveal a secret, and to give myself some privacy to think.

Ever since Henry and I became engaged, it's been wedding *this* and wedding *that*. We've been sorting through guests lists, budgets, invitations, the legalities of marriage, and even moving. Of course, I'm the only one doing any moving, since Henry has the nicer apartment.

And in New York City, apartments are do or die.

As I climb to the crest of the hill, I feel the true weight of my decision settling on my shoulders. In my fantasies, my perfect man was never Henry. It was the quiet librarian at the New York Public Library that I've never talked to before. Or it was the stunning, gentlemanly man who'd helped me catch the taxi that almost drove off with my purse. When you don't know the man, you can make up any personality you want. Henry doesn't have many of the qualities of the perfect man.

Of *my* perfect man.

He's arrogant, brash, and rude to waiters. But he tips generously anyway. Though I'm not sure if that's because he is generous, or if he likes to flash his money. An investor and entrepreneur, Henry built up his empire in his early twenties. I've been there since the beginning, and we were close at first. But the more successful he became, the more he changed.

The sun is warm on my bare shoulders and the air smells faintly of freshly mown grass and lavender. Behind me, I can hear the sounds of the wedding, conversation, laughter, the tinkling of music. Henry footed the entire bill, with a few contributions from me. As a librarian at an inner-city high school, my salary would never have colored this extravagant affair. But it's what Henry wanted. And, I'll admit, it does feel like a fairytale. But I'm not sure if Henry is my prince.

Suddenly, the breeze picks up considerably, sending a chill through me. I wrap my arms around myself, bouquet in hand. The leaves in the nearby oak trees rustle loudly. It sounds like whispering.

I sigh and turn away from the mansion, facing instead towards the city. I can't see New York from here, but I can imagine it. The gentle park and woods here are so different from the hustle and bustle of the city. A cloud passes over the sun, casting a long shadow over me.

A dark shadow.

I toss the bouquet between my hands. Maybe the sudden change in the weather is a bad omen, a sign that I shouldn't go through with this. I'll feel terrible if I bail on Henry. My family will still be in trouble if I do, and he'll probably resent me for the rest of our lives. I don't want to think about what a man with his kind of money could do if I made him angry.

Tara will be here soon to escort me to the ceremony. I never thought getting married would be so difficult for me. The shadow over me stretches forward and swirls. Odd for a cloud. I look up and see blue sky above me, and then black closing in on me.

Fear grips my gut as a giant, black creature descends from the sky. Its wings stretch out impossibly long, as wide as the hill. And it reaches out a clawed bird's foot towards me. A scream lodges in my throat as I look into its eyes.

Hazel eyes set into a panther's face.

I'm hallucinating. The stress and pressure of the wedding has finally gotten to me and my brain is responding by creating a hallucination of a monster. *That has to be it.*

Because monsters aren't real.

Something like this *can't* be real.

I stumble backwards, tripping over the tulle of my gown. One of my sparkling heels falls off, but I don't reach for it because the monster is close. In seconds, that clawed foot is wrapped around me, squeezing me tightly. Finally, the scream frees itself from my throat and shatters through the silence. I drop my bouquet as the ground falls away. When I'm high over the tree line, supported only by the beast's foot, I let my fear overtake me.

Darkness claims me.

CHAPTER 3

ALTAIR

I peer through the open balcony door studying the woman lying unconscious on the ornate rug.

After snatching her from the hilltop and bringing her through the portal into my world, I placed her into one of the many empty rooms in the palace. Even if she is to eventually bind herself to me and commit her life to mine, I don't think it's appropriate to force her to live in my room.

Not yet anyway.

When I saw her on that hill, wringing her hands, dressed in such finery, I knew that she was the one. I could smell the Bloodbane witch in her veins even from the sky.

My claws grip the stone of the palace easily as I cling to the exterior walls, watching. Navi has come and gone several times, checking to make sure the woman is in good health. I cock my head, tail swishing in the open air, and study the woman.

She is beautiful, almost as beautiful as Maaz. Certainly not as wicked looking. She's petite, and a little too thin for my tastes, but despite her small size her breasts are full. Her light brown hair has been swept into a low bun and decorated with white flowers. I wonder if this is the style in the human realm. She stirs softly, a low moan escaping her full lips.

The sun streams in through the open balcony door, falling on her dark lashes. As they open, I can see that in the sunlight, her blue eyes turn a vibrant shade of turquoise.

I suck in a ragged breath.

She is beautiful.

Stunning.

Captivating.

And I can't look away. I also can't believe that the key to ending my curse is in this room. That she is living and breathing and only a few feet from me.

She rises slowly from the floor, propping herself up on her hands as she stares in confusion around the room. The ivory gown she wears clings to her attractively, rustling with the slightest movements. I almost purr at the sight of her.

Suddenly, her head snaps towards me and she screams, a shrill cry that sends me hissing. The woman scrambles to her feet and lunges towards the door. The door that Navi has already locked. She bangs against it, staring wild-eyed at me over her shoulder.

"Help me! Let me out!" She screams, her fists pounding against the door.

I'm not surprised by her reaction. As the beast, I am terrifying to behold. Enormous and a wicked combination of several intimidating creatures rolled into one. But for some reason, I am angered by it. Many a woman has seen my beast form and clawed away, yet seeing *this* woman lurching away from me bristles my ego and wounds me in ways I care not to admit.

If she thinks I am a monster, I'll behave as one.

I snarl and leap from the wall to the balcony. I can barely fit my large frame onto it, but the claws of my bird's feet keep me secured on the railing.

"Silence," I growl.

Her eyes stretch impossibly wide at the sound of my voice. The color drains from her face. "You can talk."

"Of course, I can talk." I narrow my eyes at her. "Now, stop screaming, or I'll feed you to the wild dogs. Better yet, I'll eat you myself."

I would never do either, but anger forces the words out of me.

Her jaw goes slack and then she grabs at the door handle, shaking it vigorously. "Someone help me!"

I hiss, leaning my head further into the room.

Suddenly, pain lances through my forehead and a book clatters to the floor at my feet. "S-stay away from me!" The woman warns, another book in her hand.

I almost laugh at her feisty nature but remember myself. "You dare strike me?"

She grunts and launches another book. I dodge in time, and the book collides with the stone wall behind me. "Don't come any closer!" She shouts, her voice trembling.

I snarl viciously at her and snap my powerful jaws. "Suit yourself, mortal."

With a final growl, I launch myself off of the balcony and into the sky. I free fall for a moment, just long enough to enjoy the wind rushing through my fur before I stretch out my wings. The large wings catch the wind with a jolt. I glide through the sky, circling the castle once.

Below me, my guards and servants are busy with activity. The news of the woman's arrival has spread quickly. I worry that my people will put too much faith in us. I spot Navi in the courtyard below, she waves.

Slowly, I descend. My great wings beat against the wind to fight against gravity until my feet touch the stones of the courtyard. I prowl towards Navi, rolling out my shoulders. She watches me appraisingly.

"What is it?" I ask.

"I wonder if it's wise to keep the woman here," Navi says bluntly.

If I could cock a brow at her, I would. "What do you mean? Where else would be keep the woman who could save my people?"

"I mean, I wonder if it was wise to bring her here at all. She doesn't appear to be a Bloodbane witch. Or a witch at all." She pauses. "I fear the scholars may have made a mistake."

"She is the one Navi, I can smell it on her," I purr.

Navi mulls over this. "It will be challenging."

"Is she still throwing a tantrum?" I sit, my tail flicking out languidly behind me.

"She calmed down after you left. I heard weeping."

If my heart weren't so cold and if I hadn't lived for so many years, I might have pitied the woman. But my people's plight is far worse than hers. "I will visit her tonight."

Navi sighs, her hand gripped around the hilt of her sheathed sword. "Be careful, Altair."

"Why?" I stretch. "Worried the little mortal will break my me?"

Navi says nothing, but her eyes tell me all that I need to know. I rise and stalk past her, the claws of my feet clicking on the stone. Navi always was too over-protective of me. She strides away towards the soldier's barracks and I watch her stiff back. She was there the night Maaz cursed me. And I know she feels responsible for what happened. Even in a thousand years she hasn't forgiven herself.

Night is falling, the sun dripping over the horizon like molten gold. I feel a tinge of nerves in my stomach at the thought of meeting the woman in person for the first time. Mortals know very little of my realm and of magic, they think the Fae are children's stories. And they think witches are pagans.

She must believe me.

I *need* her to believe me. To trust me.

Or my entire world will pay the price.

As the last drop of sunlight fades, my body transforms from the winged beast to my Fae form in a cloud of smoke. Maaz always was very theatrical. I brush off my black tunic, and a feather floats to the ground. I grind it beneath my foot before heading back to the castle.

Outside the woman's room, I pause in front of a mirror and study myself. I run a hand over my black hair, tucking loose strands back into place. Dressed in an obsidian tunic and pants, I wonder if I look too intimidating.

I am Altair, King of the Fae.

Intimidating is my personal preference.

I wait and listen. The woman is silent behind the door, but I catch the soft sounds of her breath. She seems calmer now.

Good. Because we don't have much time for her to ready herself.

Without knocking, I throw the door open and stride into the room. The woman is on the bed, sleeping. She must have tired herself out with all the crying and raging. I pause over her. She looks harmless while she sleeps. I reach a hand out to tuck a stray strand of light brown hair out of her face instinctively.

Suddenly, her hand is at my wrist, gripping it tightly. She tugs it, jerking it to the side and tossing my arm away. Off balance, I stumble, just as she lunges from the bed. She sprints for the door, but I'm in front of her in an instant. She gasps, surprised by my speed. I grin down at her, my hazel eyes flashing with rage.

She darts around me, but my hand is there to catch her. I wrap my arm around her waist as she struggles against me.

"Let me go, bastard!" She snarls.

I drag her back towards the bed and she squirms more fiercely. But I'm stronger than her and I'm faster than her. She could never escape me. With a grunt, I lift her from the ground and toss her carelessly onto the bed. She yelps, bouncing softly and then scrambles to the edge, as if to run again.

"Not so fast," I growl, pushing her back onto the mattress.

She glares fearfully at me as I pin her down. Straddling her now, my knees are on either side of her waist, my hands pinning her arms around her head. She turns to the side, exposing that delicious, porcelain neck. I swallow with some difficulty as I resist the urge to run my tongue along the nape of her perfect skin.

As if she can sense my inclination, she snaps her head towards me. Her eyes meet mine, fierce and fiery. She studies my face, the scowl on her lips deepening as she takes in my features. I squeeze her wrists tightly and she winces. Her eyes drift to my pointed ears. Surprised, she sucks in a sharp breath, her chest rising. My gaze drops to her chest, to the cleavage visible above the neckline of her gown. Beautiful, flawless skin. I growl, instinct demanding that I claim her for myself. At the sound, her eyes go wide and fearful.

"I won't hurt you," I say, forcing some semblance of kindness into my voice.

"You're hurting me right now," she retorts, clenching her hands into fists.

"Because you were trying to escape." I tilt my head towards the open door. "Though I don't know where you would go. You certainly wouldn't get far. My guards are all around and the palace is a very, very big place."

"Where am I? Who are you?" She raises her voice, struggling against me again. "What am I doing here?" I push away from her, releasing her arms and slipping off the bed in one swift move. She sits up, watching me apprehensively as I shut the door.

I gesture to one of the arm chairs by the fireplace and incline my head.

She purses her lips and lifts her chin. "I'm fine over here."

"Sit." I say, grabbing the back of the chair and squeezing the fabric tightly.

"No thank you."

I narrow my eyes at her, "It isn't a request."

Stiffly, she stomps towards me and throws herself into the armchair. She crosses her arms and looks pointedly away from me. "I want to go home. Take me back. Away from... whatever this place is."

"No," I say, slinging an ankle over my knee.

"Why the fuck not?"

I lounge back, enjoying the way her brows furrow with anger. "What is your name, female?"

"My god, you don't even know my name?" She scoffs. "Why would you send that monster after me if you don't even know my name?"

My brows raise in surprise. So, she hasn't realized that the beast and I are one. *Good, that gives us time.* "Just tell me your name."

She meets my gaze defiantly. "Verity. Verity Chastain."

"Verity," I say, tasting her name. Against her own desires, she blushes. "It's a beautiful name."

Verity. The key to ending this curse. *My curse.*

She isn't how I pictured her, and I imagined our first meeting differently, though I'm not sure what I expected. Of course, she's well within her rights to be upset at having been ripped away from her life and brought here. And it's understandable that she would be disbelieving.

But this is her new reality.

And as cruel and unfair as it may seem, I have no inclinations to go easy on her.

CHAPTER 4

VERITY

The man with pointed ears lounges arrogantly in the armchair, watching me silently. Is he a man? I'm not sure. He looks like a man in every way except for the pointed ears and the strange light in his hazel eyes. He's also the most gorgeous man I've ever seen.

When he had me pinned on the bed, I couldn't deny that a primitive part of me imagined what it would feel like to have him rip my wedding dress off with his teeth.

Like I said—a *primitive part* of me.

The part that doesn't care that I've been kidnapped. The part that only cares that this man with the chiseled jaw and a body that is no doubt rock hard beneath all those clothes growled at me.

But I shut that down right away. The fact is, this man and whatever creature had snatched me from my wedding and brought me here were criminals. He and everyone in this castle are holding me against my will. They don't seem particularly concerned, which is infuriating.

I press my lips into an angry, thin line. "People will be looking for me. They'll find you, and when they do, they'll lock you up for a *long* time."

He snorts, a wicked grin stretching across his lips. "Charming. Though I doubt they'll find you here."

"And where is here?" I ask. Maybe I can glean some information from him and use it to escape.

"Desmarais, my capitol city," the man says, stretching his arms wide. "In the kingdom of Alnembra."

"I've never heard of Desmarais, or Alnembra," I murmur. Perhaps this man is a lunatic. So wrapped up in an elven fantasy he made up a country and even wears prosthetic elf ears. I point to his ears and waggle my finger. "Are those real?"

"Would you like to touch them?" He asks nonchalantly. "Come over here, I won't bite."

Somehow, I seriously doubt that. "I'll pass," I say. "Who are you?"

"King Altair of the House Ranul. You can call me Altair." He dips his chin in a shallow bow.

I cock a brow disbelievingly. "A King? Really? That's what you're going with? It's your fantasy I guess. I love how dedicated you are to your character, it's truly admirable. But I'd like to end this game of pretend now."

Altair barks a laugh. "Fantasy? Pretend? Oh, Verity, darling, you couldn't be further from the truth."

Darling? I bristle at the condescending tone to his deep voice. "You can't honestly expect me to believe that elves are real? And that I'm in some magical, fantasy kingdom?"

"Fae, actually," he snaps, narrowing his eyes. "Fae, not elves. Elves are so… commercial."

I roll my eyes. "What am I doing here? Couldn't you have picked someone else to play pretend with you?"

Altair's eyes darken. "No, actually. It could only be you."

"Why?" I ask, curiosity piqued.

His lips press tightly closed and he scowls. "Enough. No more questions. All you need to know is that you will remain here. I will not return you to the mortal realm."

I laugh softly, but the sound is humorless. Either I'm being held hostage by an insane cosplayer, or I'm hallucinating. There can be no other option. I refuse to believe that elves, or Fae—whatever they're called—are real. It's simply impossible.

I'm a librarian, knowledge is my greatest strength. Even children know that elves aren't real. I believed in them when I was a kid, but I've grown up since then. I don't make houses for the fairies in my backyard anymore. I don't picture elves running through the trees beside my car when I drive through the forest. This is insanity.

"I'm hallucinating, that's the best option, right?" I murmur, mostly to myself. Altair cocks his head at me, listening. "Because if I'm hallucinating that means I'm not kidnapped, and insane cosplayers didn't create a giant animatronic bird to capture me. Because that's just crazy."

"Animatronic?" Altair mutters.

"And if I'm not kidnapped, then that means I'll wake up soon. Preferably on the hill, with minutes to spare before my wedding," I continue, ignoring him. "And no one will be the wiser. No one even has to know I had a stress-induced hallucination."

"Your wedding," Altair echoes. His voice is as cold as ice and sends a chill through me.

"Yes. I was supposed to get married today. So take me back," I demand, though my voice warbles with uncertainty.

Do I really want to go back? Is this hallucination like a wake-up call for me—a realization that Henry is not the one for me? And if it's a kidnapping, am I actually lucky? I purse my lips thoughtfully; I could always use the kidnapping as an excuse to break up with Henry. No one could blame me if I did that. But what kind of person would that make me? The kind that can't take responsibility for their own feelings.

Altair's eyes are like a razor-sharp blade piercing through my chest. I thought he looked dangerous before, but now, there's a murderous gaze in his eyes. He picks at his nails. "You don't sound particularly enthused, perhaps you should be thanking me?"

No, I can't back out of my wedding. Henry is a good man, mostly. And my parents need me to do this for them. "I am enthusiastic," I argue, forcing a grin. "But being kidnapped has killed the mood. Take me back."

Altair loses all semblance of nonchalance. He leans forward, baring his teeth at me. "You may as well forget about your groom because you are never going back. You're mine now, do you understand?"

Rage floods through me, followed by painful sorrow. "You won't get away with this, you can't keep me here!" I shout, balling my tulle skirt in my fists.

Altair rises, looming over me. "I do what I will," he says, his voice dangerously soft. I freeze at the tone, some instinct in me forcing me to clamp down like a rabbit in a hawk's gaze.

He turns on his heel and stalks from the room. I can see the rage broiling off of him. The door slams shut in his wake, and I hear the lock click from the other side. Trapped here. Exhaustion sweeps through me, quelling some of my rage and fear. If he had wanted to hurt me, he would have done it already. But I don't trust him.

I drop my head against the blue suede of the armchair, staring morosely at the fireplace. My room is several stories off the ground, and the castle appears to be built on a cliff side. If I tried to escape through the window, chances are good I would fall to my death.

And, of course, waltzing out the door isn't an option. Altair said there were many guards. I bet he has some posted outside my door right now. And if I were to run, he wouldn't be far behind. He's fast, impossibly fast. But maybe that's because he's Fae.

My lips spread into a grin at the thought. In my fatigue, I had actually almost started to believe his ludicrous story. If it were true, and I was in another dimension—or another realm as he called it—I would never find my own way back to New York again. I wonder vaguely if time passes differently here. Maybe I've already been gone for three years.

I shake my head, forcing the thought away. Speculation won't help. I drop my eyes to my wedding dress, to the lace and tulle that's torn and frayed after a day of raging and the brief scuffle I had with Altair.

Tears prick at my eyes, but I blink them back. I can't cry. I can only imagine how upset my parents and Tara must be. My parents were so looking forward to the wedding. Henry is their idea of a golden boy, the perfect son-in-law. And Tara is probably worried sick. She would know that I wouldn't run away without telling her.

Henry… I curl in on myself, thinking of how angry he must have been when I never appeared for the ceremony. I'm sure after a few days of fury, he'll come around. He'll realize that something must have happened to me. And if I do find a way home, he'll take me back. I hope.

But I can't sit around in this wedding dress any longer. I fumble with the zipper in the back but finally manage to tug it down. I step out of it and carefully drape it over the arm chair Altair was sitting in. After rummaging through a dresser, I find a man's shirt. The same style that Altair was wearing. It's loose and airy, with two strings at the neckline to tie together.

If I'm to get out of here, and I need to get out of here, then I'll have to somehow convince Altair to trust me. Once he trusts me, maybe he'll reveal how I got here and how to get back. He'll give me more freedom and leeway, which is exactly what I need. Altair is my ticket out.

After some thought, I drag a wooden chair in front of the door and prop it under the handle. They can keep my locked in but perhaps I can keep them locked out. Satisfied, and feeling a little safer, I slip under the covers of the king-sized bed and roll to face the door. Blinking sleepily, my eyes grow heavier each time they slip closed. Sleep takes me swiftly, and I dream about Altair.

CHAPTER 5

I spread my wings, relishing the warmth of the sunlight on my feathers as I soar over Desmarais. Perhaps Navi was right about Verity. Perhaps she isn't the key to ending the curse. I bank sharply left until I'm facing the castle. She's there, inside her room. What she's thinking only the Gods know. Though I can assume with some certainty she's thinking of her beloved fiancé. I snarl at the thought of the man I've never met.

I snarl because he has claimed her heart. Because if her heart belongs to another, she will be hard-pressed to do what she must to save my kingdom. I don't want to fly too close to the castle, in case I see her on her balcony. I know the sight of her will tempt me to stop and speak with her. But I don't want to hear anything more about her marriage, or her demands to return to the mortal realm.

She can't go back without my help, something I suspect she has figured out. The mortal realm is connected to this one through a portal that only the strongest of the Fae can summon. But we don't often attend the human world. They die so quickly, and their conflicts are so petty, the Fae tire of them easily.

Verity is one of the first humans to step foot into this world. There was a legend that a man once wandered into this realm. He wandered throughout the Fae lands for a time before discovering the Bloodbane witch clans. No one saw him again.

I spy a shadow against one of the windows in Verity's room and turn away from it. I dive towards the ground. I streak past the castle walls and then the face of the cliff, towards the buildings below. At the last minute, I stretch my wings and catch myself. The air billows me upwards, back to soaring height.

I remember when I first became this beast. I felt like an infant learning to walk and speak all over again. It took years to master flying. But I've grown to enjoy it, even if it means I appear like a gruesome cat-bird creature.

A foul wind blows from the west. I glance towards the mountain range. Deep within it, Maaz and her covens camp, living off of the wild beasts the goods they raid from the Fae. I narrow my eyes and fly towards the high peaks. A wind like that is often an omen, an accompanying sign to the approach of the witches.

I have my men patrolling our border with the Bloodbane witches constantly, they report to Navi daily. But with the end of the thousand years approaching, I suspect Maaz and her cohorts will grow more brazen. Sometimes I join my soldiers in their patrol. I'm useless during the day otherwise. Stuck in this beastly form, I can't attend to matters of state. And the knowledge of my curse has only made neighboring kingdoms distance themselves from me. I sneer. No one wants to associate with an enemy of Maaz. Cowards.

Finally, once I've flown past the last of the villages, I spy smoke from a firepit curling into the sky. I circle, peering down through the sparse trees to the rocky ground below. Suddenly, an arrow streaks past me, nearly impaling one of my wings.

I snarl and dive to the ground. Bloodbane witches coat the tips of their red-fletched arrows in poison. I land heavily, my claws scraping against the stony ground. Three Bloodbane witches stand before me, bows drawn back. They release their arrows in unison, I dodge to the left, using my tail to move more nimbly.

Eyes bright and deadly, I lunge for them. My paw slams into one of the witches, sending her flying into a nearby tree. She crumples at the base of the trunk, whimpering. I turn my attention to the other two, snarling with delight.

Fighting was always one of my greatest strengths. But there's really nothing that can compare to slicing an enemy open with your bare hands. Something so raw and primal, I wonder if Maaz merely drew this beast out of me as if it were always there. Blood coats my claws as I drag them through one of the witch's chest. Her body spasms and she pales with fear. Or perhaps that's the blood loss. When the last of my claws slips from her torso, she keels over and lands with a hollow thud. The witch I tossed against the tree is waking, groaning softly. I circle the third witch, my eyes on the blade in her hand.

I'm surprised none of them have used any spells against me yet. Perhaps they're young and inexperienced. Weak. I snap my teeth at her, enjoying the way she flinches back. But her lips are set into a furious grimace.

"What are you doing so far into my lands?" I hiss.

She grips the blade tighter. "Soon to be ours," she retorts. Her voice is husky and rough, like gravel. It's at odds with her youthful face. Perhaps she isn't as young as I thought.

"You Bloodbane witches are getting ahead of yourselves." Rage coils in my chest. "These lands are mine until the curse claims me."

She laughs mirthlessly. "You're weak, King. You'll never break Maaz's curse, even with that pretty little mortal holed up in your castle."

My blood runs cold at her words. Navi and I have instructed the servants and soldiers at the palace to keep Verity's existence a secret. If Maaz were to know how close we are to breaking the curse, I have no doubt she would kill Verity.

"I suppose your people aren't as loyal as you thought," the witch cackles.

I narrow my eyes at her. So, one of my own is a spy for the Bloodbane witches. Navi and I will find them quickly, and I'll kill them myself. Before the witch can speak another word, I pounce on her and close my jaws over her throat. Her bones snap easily, like a dry branch. I drop her limp body unceremoniously and pad towards the remaining witch.

She struggles to her feet, a dark bruise forming on her temple. "You," I purr. "I have a job for you."

"Go to Hell," she spits.

I chuckle. "With the rest of your kind?" With a flick of my tail, I drive the witch to the ground. Before she can scramble away, I pin her down with a paw. "You'll take a message to Maaz for me," I hiss.

She pales as I lengthen my claws, letting them prick her chest. Blood wells and she winces. "What is it?"

"Very good, I knew you were smarter than you look," I quip. "Tell Maaz to stay the fuck out of my lands. Tell her I won't tolerate any more incursions like this one. Tell her that I tire of her impatience."

The witch glowers but nods stiffly. I pull away, letting her rise to her feet. The witch's greasy hair hangs in matted locks over her face, almost hiding the bruise. She tugs her dress tighter over her blood-stained chest.

"Think you can remember all that?" I ask.

She nods.

"Then go," I hiss, swatting at her.

She turns and disappears into thin air. Probably magicking herself to Maaz, or as close as she can get. Teleportation magic isn't easy, and it takes a lot of energy. Maybe that's why none of the witches used any spells during our short skirmish—they were conserving energy for their retreat.

I stare emotionless down at the bodies. The witches won't return for them, they never do. So, the animals will eat them. I take off, my wings spraying dust and leaves over the witch's corpses. I head directly back to the castle, the witch's words about the spy echoing through my mind.

I can't let anything or anyone risk exposing Verity and destroying my one chance at breaking free from Maaz. I find Navi in the practice yard beside the soldier's barracks, training. I drop to the ground in a clear space free of Fae and equipment and wait for her to approach. I learned a long time ago not to disturb Navi during her training.

I wait, basking in the sunshine. With a final blow to her opponent, she drives him to the ground, her glaive poised over him. Breathing heavily, she pulls back and swings the glaive in an arc overhead before bringing to rest at her side. Her auburn hair shimmers in the sunlight as she bows sharply to her opponent. He slinks away, defeated.

"What is it, Your Majesty?" Navi asks, striding towards me.

"In private," I say.

She nods, leaving the barracks as I propel myself into the sky. I skim over the roofs of the stables towards a clearing where Navi and I won't be overheard. She arrives a moment later, glaive gone. I pace, tail swishing agitatedly.

"There is a spy in the palace," I say, keeping my voice low.

Her brows raise in surprise. "A spy?"

"I was patrolling the borders when I found a small group of Bloodbane witches. One of them knew about Verity," I explain.

"Are you sure it wasn't simply to goad information from you?" Navi asks.

"She said 'mortal.'" I shake my head. "They know."

"I'll have my best men on this, Altair," Navi says, reaching a hand out to comfort me. I let her rest her palm on my neck for a moment before pulling away. "We'll find the spy."

"Bring them to me once you've found them." I turn my glittering eyes to her. "So, they know what they've done."

Navi dips her head in a bow before marching out of the clearing. I trust her to find the betrayer. Navi has been a loyal companion to me for many years, and her skills are unparalleled. I watch as her figure recedes and then sigh heavily.

"What's this about spies?" I hear a melodic voice behind me.

I pivot, eyes narrowed at Verity. She leans casually against the stone wall surrounding the palace, eyeing me. Dressed in trousers and a loose-fitting shirt, she looks more at ease than she did in her wedding gown. If I find where she keeps it, I may tear it to shreds so I never have to look at it again. She tosses her light brown hair behind her shoulder and glares.

"What did you hear?" I ask, suspicion lacing my voice. I pace towards her and she tries to take a step back but stumbles.

She catches herself before she falls. "Don't come at me looking like you're going to eat me," she snaps, crossing her arms over her chest.

"Don't eavesdrop on my conversations," I retort, stopping a few feet away from her.

"It wasn't intentional." Verity rolls her eyes. "So, why are there spies in the palace?"

"It's none of your concern," I say.

Verity shrugs. "Well, as far as I know, I am the only 'mortal' here." She gestures with four of her fingers when she says the word 'mortal'. "So, it's about me, isn't it?"

I yawn, my jaw stretching widely. "What are you doing out of your room?"

"What, are you going to drag me back there so I can wait for Altair to harass me again?" She crosses her arms over her chest. "Navi said I could get some fresh air."

"Harass?" I plop down on the grass to rest.

Fatigue settles into my bones as I relax. These past few days I haven't managed to find much time to sleep. And when I have, I never seem to get any rest. My thoughts are always on the curse, and more recently, on Verity. But the sun is warm on my back and the grass is soft. It's comfortable here. Even with Verity glowering at me.

"He's infuriating. He won't even tell me why I'm here," she complains.

Her blue eyes turn on me, sparkling. I can see the cogs turning in her head as her brows furrow. My little mortal thinks she can pull the wool over my eyes. I grin under her gaze. This is going to be fun.

CHAPTER 6

I throw open the doors of the wardrobe in my room in search of something to wear. Inside, I find a myriad of simple dresses and intricate gowns, but no pants. I wrinkle my nose at the selection. Long skirts don't seem like the best choice for a woman who's been kidnapped by strangers. Even if those strangers might just be elves.

I turn away, closing the doors softly. The cool air tickles my bare legs and I curl my toes into the soft rug. Anything will do. That is, anything that won't slow me down if I need to run. Sighing, I open the dresser I found this shirt in and rummage through it. In the bottom drawer, I find several pairs of carefully folded linen trousers. I unfold a pair and hold it up, studying it.

With no zipper, the pants are laced with a string. Shrugging, I tug them on and bunch the waist band in my fist, so the pants don't fall to the ground. The lacing is tricky, but I manage to tie it tight enough to keep them at my hips at least. With a little more digging I find a belt to cinch around my waist.

I study myself in the mirror. Dark brown trousers that bunch around my feet with the extra length. A thin white shirt that's three sizes too big. And I think I can see the faint blush coloring of my nipples. Frowning, I grab a gray shirt from the dresser and tug it on over my head. Without a bra, I'll feel more comfortable in dark colors.

Satisfied, I roll up the hem of my pants a few times so I can walk without tripping. There's a sharp rap at my door and then it shakes the chair stops it from opening. I smirk, glad my little trick worked.

"Verity," I hear a woman say through the door. "Move the barricade. I don't want to break the door down."

I roll my eyes but do as she says. It would be worse to be without a door. I set the heavy chair aside with a huff and then cross my arms over my chest. The woman, Fae, enters, turning her green eyes to me. I count the knives she has strapped to her body, including her sword. Eight. I eye her suspiciously, it seems excessive. She watches me like a cat stalking a mouse. She's tall and willowy, with auburn hair and almond-shaped eyes. Dressed in form-fitting trousers and a leather cuirass over a linen tunic, she's clearly a warrior.

"Who are you?" I ask, taking a hesitant step backwards.

"Navi, Captain of the Guard." She dips her chin, though her eyes never leave me. She certainly looks it. "How did you sleep?"

I shrug. "Fine." In truth, I slept like a baby, despite my fear that Altair would break down the door in the middle of the night and ravish me.

She nods, satisfied. "If you're hungry, I can take you to the dining hall."

"I'm not hungry," I say quickly. I don't think I would be able to eat anyway, not with the stress of the kidnapping and Altair's strange claims about dimensions and realms.

"How would you like to see more of the castle? Or perhaps the grounds?" Navi's hand drifts to the hilt of her blade.

I have no doubt she and the other elves would be watching me closely. I don't relish the thought of putting myself out in the open, surrounded by dangerous strangers. But if I stay any longer in the room, I might go mad. I might be able to search for a way out.

"I would love to see the grounds." I smile as sincerely as I can.

Navi cocks a brow. "Humans are so amusing," she murmurs, eyeing me.

"What do you mean?" I follow her out of the room and down the hall.

My eyes widen as I take in the architecture of the palace. Even the halls are designed and built beautifully. With arched ceilings and thin engaged columns sculpted with flowering vines. Gold frames house elegant oil paintings displayed along the hall, and a soft, green carpet runs the length of it. Navi doesn't notice my admiration of the building. I can only imagine what the rest of the palace might look like.

"You think you're clever," Navi says in response to my question. "You're hoping to find the route to exit the palace and then explore the grounds for another way out. You suspect I'm merely being hospitable, but in reality, I was simply curious."

It doesn't faze me that Navi has guessed my intentions, so I don't try to deny it. "Curious about what?"

"What kind of woman you are," she says simply as she waves at the guards to open a set of tall, double doors. "I was hoping for something a little more... intricate."

I purse my lips. "I'm sorry to disappoint."

"This is where I leave you, I have training to attend to." Navi turns to me, pausing in the doorway. "I'll have Fae watching you wherever you go with instructions to stop you, using force if necessary. Please don't do anything rash."

"Wait!" I bound down the steps after Navi. "I want to talk to Altair."

"His Majesty is indisposed," Navi quips.

I wrap my hand around her elbow, to stop her from walking away from me. "I don't care, tell me where he is. I need to talk to him." At the very least, I want to find out what he wants from me. I just want to go home.

Navi's eyes drop to her elbow, still in my hand. Immediately, I regret latching onto her. Suddenly, she twists away from me in a blur of motion. I stumble backwards but she catches me, an arm wrapped around me to my back. I feel a sharp tinge of pain as she rests a dagger against my throat. Her face is close, only inches from mine as she bends over me.

"Put your hand on me again and I'll cut it off," she breathes.

I nod, eyes wide. She tosses me aside, sheathing the blade in a single smooth motion. I watch, my gut as cold as ice, as she stalks away and disappears around another building. It isn't until I'm sure she's gone that I realize I've been holding my breath.

I pant, bending over and propping my hands on my knees. I've never been so afraid before in my life, not even when that bird-creature poked its jaguar head into my room. Perhaps because that was so unbelievable.

I glance over my shoulder, in the direction she disappeared. I have no doubt that Navi wouldn't hesitate to fulfill her warning. My hands are trembling as the adrenaline abates, I try to recover my breathing. Even in New York, I wouldn't expect a threat like that. I've run into muggers on the street before, but somehow, a switchblade in their hand is less frightening than in Navi's.

Calm again, I spin in a slow circle and take in my surroundings. The castle is a giant monolith of gray stone, turrets and buttresses and towers skewering the sky. And all around it wraps a tall, stone wall. There are a few side buildings, I can identify one as the stables, but the others I'm not sure of. I wander away from the front entrance, towards a manicured hedge. It leads to a private garden filled with red roses. In the center is a small fountain, with a statue of a koi fish spurting arcs of water into the air.

I spend the next hours walking along the wall, searching for places I can climb or secret entrances. But the only entrance I find is the main one at the end of the long, treed drive. And that's protected by a heavy wooden gate and a guardhouse.

I avoid doing anything more than running my hand along the wall, in case the Fae trailing me mistake any of my movements for an escape attempt. I'm not interested in being shot with an arrow. But I avoid heading in the direction Navi went, so I steer clear of the walls nearest the palace.

A shadow streaks overhead, too fast to be a cloud, and too large to be a bird. I look up, blocking the bright rays of the sun with my hand and see the creature flying past. It heads towards the buildings I haven't explored yet and disappears. I furrow my brows. Maybe it was a trick of the light, but I thought I saw its claws were painted red.

Moments later, it appears again. I shrink back into the trees lining the drive as he descends into a copse of trees on the other side, near the wall. Navi joins him a moment later, her eyes narrowed. So, the beast knows the Captain of the Guard. But, why would the two of them meet in such a strange place? Will Altair join them? I wonder.

Curious, I scurry over the road and onto the lawn on the other side. Running on my tiptoes, I ignore the Fae guards following me. When they see where I'm headed, they fall back. Probably because they know I'm not liable to escape directly where the creature and Navi are. I creep through the trees towards the sounds of their voices.

"We'll find the spy," I hear Navi say, her voice short and clipped.

Spy? My brows furrow.

The creature speaks, its deep voice carrying over the breeze. "Bring them to me once you've found them. So, they know what they've done."

Silence falls, and I hear Navi moving away. I shrink back against the trunk of a tree, so she doesn't see me. After a moment, I peek around the tree and into the clearing. The creature is alone now, Navi is gone. Carefully, I approach, one hand on the wall. The beast is sitting in the clearing, staring up at the sky. His feathers ruffle slightly in the summer breeze.

I summon my courage and bravado. "What's this about spies?"

The creature whirls on me, his teeth bared, golden eyes bright and alert. He pauses when he recognizes me. "What did you hear?" He asks, pacing towards me.

Panic flares within me as he approaches, slinking like a predator. I take a step backwards but bump into the wall and stumble. Regaining my footing, I glower at him. "Don't come at me looking like you're going to eat me." My heart is raging in my chest, that's the second time today I've felt like I've endured a near-death experience.

He pauses at my words, tail flicking out sharply. "Don't eavesdrop on my conversations."

So, he can at least listen. When he wants. "It wasn't intentional," I lie. "So, why are there spies in the palace?"

I expect something along the lines of political intrigue. Perhaps Altair has a half-brother vying for the throne. Or maybe Fae journalists have snuck into the castle to catch the latest news on his kidnapping tendencies.

To my surprise, the creature drops my gaze. "It's none of your concern."

"Well, as far as I know, I am the only 'mortal' here." I bend my fingers in air quotes, he wrinkles his velvet nose in confusion. "So, it's about me, isn't it?"

He ignores me, yawning lazily. Carelessly. "What are you doing out of your room?"

I scowl. He's treating me like a prisoner. A prisoner he doesn't feel particularly concerned about, but a prisoner, nonetheless. "What, are you going to drag me back there so I can wait for Altair to harass me again?" I toss my hair over my shoulder and cross my arms over my chest defensively. "Navi said I could get some fresh air."

The creature lies on the grass, stretching out his paws. I glance at the claws; they are covered in blood. It wasn't a trick of the light. I feel my stomach turn at the sight. "He's infuriating. He won't even tell me why I'm here." I try to hide the fearful warble in my voice with whining.

He lolls his head to the side lazily, as if he couldn't care less what Altair does or doesn't tell me. I eye him, considering the situation. From what I've seen so far, this creature has as much power as Altair. After all, Navi listens to them both. But it was the creature who first spoke to me, even before Altair came to me.

He seems kinder, more open to my thoughts. And while it's strange that I can find a cat-bird monster such as this personable, he's much more approachable than Altair. Maybe that's just because Altair's looks are distracting. And make me think wicked things.

I shake my head imperceptibly, trying to collect my thoughts. I need to stay focused on the situation at hand. With someone—or thing—like this creature at my side, I could have more protection from Altair. And maybe he would even help me escape. If I play my cards right.

The creature grins at me, which is disconcerting since it has the face of a black jaguar. I resist the urge to shudder. Instead, I sink to the ground a few feet away from him and lean back against the wall. "What should I call you?" I ask.

He considers my question for a moment. "Acubens," he finally says just as I'm about to press him further.

"And you are male, right?" I gesture towards him. He sounds male to me, but what do I know about fairytale creature anatomy.

He chuckles the sound vibrating through the earth. "I am, would you like to see?"

I grimace. "I'll take your word for it."

Acubens flares his wings and beats them gently before laying them out to rest in the sun. He rests his head on his paws. "Any other questions?"

"Besides the overarching one of what I'm doing here?" I sigh. "So many."

"Since I'm nice," he yawns. "I'll answer three of your questions as well as I can."

"Very generous." I smile sarcastically. "How long do I have to stay here?"

"It really depends on you," he says slyly.

I wait for more, but he starts licking at his paws. "That's it?" I gape. "It depends on me? Well, if that's the case then I think I'll head home right now."

"Not quite what I mean." He sighs.

"Then what do you mean?" I push, feeling irritation sparking in my chest.

"Is that your second question?" He retorts.

Damn. "No." I don't want to waste my questions.

Acubens waves a paw, as if encouraging me to go on. Maybe he's as much of a bastard as Altair is. "Anytime. I have eternity, but human lives aren't quite as long," he drawls.

I scowl at him. "Why did Altair tell you to abduct me?" Perhaps if Altair won't tell me, Acubens will.

"Mmm," he muses. "How should I explain it? Should I say he took a fancy to you? That your beauty and intelligence caught his eye? Women like those pretty lies. Or should I say that he had no real reason at all? He did it simply because he wanted to. But that's not quite right either. You'll find that no one here will answer your question, at least not as well as I have. How does it make you feel that everyone but you knows the answer to your most earnest question?"

I stare stoically at the blades of grass near my feet. I refuse to cry in front of Acubens, and certainly not because of his spiteful answer. Answer three questions? Please. I can feel his hazel eyes on me, studying my reaction.

"At least I can rule out two theories," I say, forcing myself to speak.

Acubens eyes me appraisingly. "Very good. Now, last one. And might I suggest something more light-hearted? You're far too serious."

"Will you meet with me again?" I ask. Even if he's guarded around me now, hopefully over time I can earn his trust. And then manipulate him into helping me escape. Or maybe I've read too many romance novels.

"I don't think so," he says blandly, as if he couldn't be bothered to care.

I scoff. "Why not?"

"Oh, no more questions." He turns his head away but stares at me from the corners of his eyes. "Too bad."

I rise, dusting grass and dirt off of my trousers. "Too bad."

As I stride away from him back towards the palace, I hear him purr, "Enjoy your evening, Verity."

I glance over my shoulder at him in time to see him roll onto his side and close his eyes. He looks just like a cat basking in the sun. I resist the urge to smile. He's no cat. He's an overgrown feral alley cat with chicken wings. The sun hovers just above the horizon now, and I can feel my belly aching with hunger.

Navi jogs down the steps towards me, her eyes glancing between me and the copse of trees where Acubens is hidden. She stops in front of me, green eyes raking over me. "You'll need something more appropriate for dinner."

CHAPTER 7

Altair

Silence fills the dimly lit dining hall. Typically, I don't mind silence, but somehow with Verity it stretches out between us like a taut cord ready to snap. And when it does, it will be both of us in pain. I purse my lips, slipping another bit of quail into my mouth.

Across the table, partially hidden by the vase of leaves and over-sized flowers, Verity picks at her food. "Are you enjoying the quail?" I ask, trying to sound gentle and sincere.

She lifts and drops a shoulder in a casual gesture that immediately sends a wave of frustration coursing through me. Verity doesn't even look up to meet my eyes. I growl, dropping my fork with a clatter. This is nothing new. It's been a week since I brought Verity into my realm, a week since we put all of our hopes in her. And she hasn't bothered to speak to me since the first night I met her in my human form.

Of course, she speaks to Acubens. I scowl. Acubens is the name I gave myself as the beast Maaz cursed me to be. My first inclination to tease her and use her clever plan to manipulate me against Acubens has clearly failed. If anything, I'm jealous that she feels more comfortable speaking to Acubens than to me directly. Somehow it feels like a betrayal.

I grind my teeth, watching her sip her wine. Her neglect of me doesn't appear forced whatsoever. "This can't go on forever, Verity," I murmur. "When will you tire of this?"

She finally lifts her blue eyes to meet mine. "I don't have anything to say to you unless you plan to explain your motives here."

I run my tongue over my bottom lip frustrated and catch her eyes tracking the movement. "I don't."

Maaz has prevented me from speaking of the curse to the woman who would be the key to breaking it. If I allude to it, or if anyone in my kingdom does, the curse will become permanent. And we lose all hope. So, as much as it frustrates me to keep Verity in the dark, and as much as it angers me that she hates me for something I can't control, I have to protect my people.

"Then I have nothing else to say to you," she quips.

"Then I suppose you'll just have to listen," I growl. "I know how close you've grown to Acubens this week."

She purses her lips. "And what of it?"

"Has he been more forthcoming in my motives? Or do you cling to him just to spite me?" I ask, pushing my plate aside.

"Why don't you ask him yourself? He's your pet, isn't he?" She glowers.

"Oddly enough, Acubens has been rather distant since you arrived," I lie. I watch her closely, and I don't miss the satisfied smirk that flashes across her face.

"How strange." She sips her wine nonchalantly.

I grin ferally at her. "It seems he's more your pet now."

"Jealous?" She asks, propping her chin in her hand.

My heart pounds faster at her question, at the sly way she eyes me. I've never met a woman quite like Verity. Despite the way she's been thrown into this foreign, magical world, she holds her head high. When I speak to her as Acubens, she doesn't seem even slightly afraid. She may not be a stoic warrior like Navi, but she has a strength within her.

"What if I am?" I ask, a little breathlessly. I want to hear her answer. It's been so easy to learn more about her as Acubens, I feel an indescribable pull towards her.

I know she cries when she watches some human entertainment called *The Notebook*. I know now why she refused to eat the main course two nights ago; she hates mushrooms. I know that she misses her parents, and she thinks about them every day. All day. And I know she wants to return to them. And that hurts me.

Her lips part softly at my question. "What…?"

I rise, hands pressed against the table as I lean towards her. "What if I am jealous?"

She inhales sharply and my eyes drop to her chest. "Stop it."

"Stop what?" I ask, eyes glittering.

"Stop joking around with me," she snaps. "I'm not in the mood."

My eyes flash furiously at her words. She jokes enough when I'm Acubens. I shove the vase aside, opening up the line of sight between us so I can see her more clearly. "What makes Acubens so different? Better than me?"

"He doesn't intimidate me, for one," Verity says fiercely. "He's nicer than you."

I scoff. I know I haven't intended to be kinder to her as Acubens. If anything, I've tried to be more aloof with her, knowing that she plans to manipulate Acubens for information. To pit us against each other to her advantage.

She jabs a finger at me. "See, what is that? I feel like every time I see you, you're always mocking me. These dinners are hell."

"Would you rather eat in your room?" I ask coldly, the icy feeling of rejection wrapping itself around my chest.

"I would," she retorts, eyes flashing.

A wave of anger floods through me, sending tips of my fingers tingling. "Am I really so vile?" I whisper.

I slam my chair backwards, sending it clattering to the dark marble floor. Verity flinches at the sound. I stalk around the table towards her, the flames of the fireplace illuminating my scowl. I know Verity isn't pleased to be with me. I know she suffers. But so do I.

I'm in front of her before she's had a chance to rise from her chair. She twists to face me, glowering at me as I pause in front of her. I study her. She's even more beautiful now, dressed in a wine-red silk gown that perfectly accentuates her petite frame. I swallow thickly, lost for a moment in her blue eyes.

But her scowling lips are enough to draw my mind back to the situation at hand. There's no time for her stubbornness. No time for her to foster her resentment of me. I stoop over her, propping my hands on the arm rests of her chair. I lower my face to hers, hovering only inches from her lips. Her eyes lose the furious edge as they rove over my face.

"What are you doing?" She asks softly.

She's beautiful. But she doesn't care for me. If anything, she hates me. I watch her as she fidgets under my gaze, biting her plump lips. Those lips. I can't decide if I should nibble on them or simply yell at her for frustrating me so thoroughly.

Suddenly, she drives her hands into my chest, knocking me back enough for her to squirm out from under my arms. She darts towards the door, her silk skirts tangling in her legs. "Verity, wait!" I shout, reaching for her.

But she slams the door behind her, I can hear her footsteps echoing down the hall as she runs. I drag a hand over my face, cursing myself for being too impatient. I shouldn't have loomed over her, glaring. Of course she would run.

Finally, I stalk through the door, determined to follow her. "Where did she go?" I ask the guard stationed nearby.

He points towards the entrance of the castle. I jog after her, hoping to catch her tucked away in some corner. But she's nowhere to be seen. Outside the castle, I find the gate open and the guards missing. I whirl on the soldiers who trailed me out, eyes flashing.

"What the hell is going on here?" I snarl.

The guards rush forward, inspecting the area. They drag two of my men from nearby bushes and drop them at my feet. Red-fletched arrows protrude from their necks. Navi appears at my side. She rips one of the arrows from a corpse and tosses it aside. "Bloodbane witches."

I stare out into the darkness beyond the walls of the castle. Verity is out there. "I want everyone searching for her, do you understand?" Fury and panic are welling up within me. "Find her!"

CHAPTER 8

Altair is infuriating. He's vile, sadistic, and a bully. I endure dinners with him because I'm meant to, because I don't know what they'll do to me if I don't. But every time he opens that perfectly shaped mouth, I want to slap him. And then kiss him.

God, he's driving me insane.

I sweep down the halls, nearly tripping over the long skirts of my gown. The castle may be large, but I'm feeling claustrophobic knowing that Altair is under the same roof. I just need fresh air. I shake my head, trying to forget the tingling sensation that swept through me when he bent over me. He was just trying to intimidate me; I tell myself as I push out into the night air.

It meant nothing. Whatever he wants from me, he isn't getting it. And that frustrates him. It frustrates him enough to imprison me in his arms to keep me close to him. I take a deep gulp of the night air; it smells faintly of jasmine. My core heats at the memory of his eyes on my lips. I could read his intentions in those eyes. Why did I want it so badly?

Stockholm syndrome, I realize. Of course. I've been kept here so long and treated well enough that I don't see my captors as my captors anymore. Unconsciously. I furrow my brows, considering this. I don't feel like I have Stockholm syndrome—but then again, what does it feel like?

The gravel of the main drive crunches under my shoes, the only sound on the grounds. The only sound. I stop, a few yards from the guardhouse and the main gate. It's oddly quiet. No murmurings of the guards by the gate, no night birds singing, or even crickets chirping. A cold sense of dread settles over me, and the hairs on my arms stand on end.

Something is wrong.

Suddenly, a woman materializes beside me, dressed in a blood red cloak. Beneath her deep hood, her eyes glimmer wickedly. On instinct, I step backwards, but I stumble over my dress. Her hand snakes out from the cloak and snatches my wrist before I fall.

"Let me go, who are you?" I try wrench away from her.

A second woman appears on my other side, she lifts a hand. Her nails are long and pointed, curling inwards. I open my mouth to scream as she brings her hand down and strikes me. Pain lances through my temple, and then shadows cloud my vision, the scream lodged in my throat.

When I wake, I'm on cold, hard stone. But not the stone of the castle, it's too rough for that. And too dirty. I lift my cheek from the ground, groaning as pain throbs through my skull. Bits of dirt and dust cling to my cheek, I don't bother wiping them off as I try to rise into a sitting position. I manage it, after a few tries. I shiver, cold wind from behind me rushing past me towards a light in the distance.

Where am I? There's a fire nearby, illuminating my prison. Rough stone walls arch above me with crude drawings of animals and Fae. A cave, I realize. I'm in a cave. I scoot backwards until my back is pressed against the wall, my dress snags on a rock and tears. It's a mess of dirt and rips anyway. I wrap my arms around my bare shoulders, holding myself for comfort and warmth.

There's no sign of the two women I saw before I blacked out. The light in the distance must be the entrance to the cave, is it already day? I must have been out for hours. The situation gives me a strong sense of déja vu. Though I suppose I was lucky I ended up in a castle the first time. I frown, staring into the flames of the fire, how many more times will I be kidnapped? I'm practically an expert now.

I hear footsteps echoing in the darkness of the cave, from deeper within. I turn my head sharply, heart pounding. Somehow, I'm more frightened than I was when I woke up in the castle. More frightened even than when Acubens snatched me from the hillside on my wedding day.

A woman melts out of the shadows, her hood drawn down. From her eyes, I can sense that it's the first woman I saw. She smiles sinisterly, and I imagine that all of her teeth have been sharpened into points. She moves closer to the fire, and I see it was a trick of the light. Her blonde hair is matted considerably, as if she hasn't washed in weeks, but there are no dirt smears on her pale skin. She watches me, leering, while another woman joins her.

The two of them are silent, their eyes raking over me. It sends shivers trailing up and down my spine. I feel like an animal in a slaughterhouse. Finally, one of the women speaks, "She doesn't look a thing like Maaz, does she?"

Her companion cackles. Cackles like a witch in the stories. I flinch back at the sound. "Doesn't have her courage either. Look how frightened she is, like a little mouse in a trap."

"Maaz will certainly be pleased though," the first one quips. "She'll be crowing when she sees we've brought her that stupid Fae's prized possession."

I listen as the two of them congratulate each other, eyes darting between them. It's as if they don't know I can hear them. Or they simply don't care. Whatever they are, they aren't Fae.

Their ears aren't pointed, and they lack the elegance of the Fae. Whatever these women are, they remind me of spiders.

"You would think the beast would have kept watch over her more carefully," one snorts. "It was too easy to snatch her up."

The other laughs. "The key to saving himself and his kingdom and he just lets her wander the ground alone? If that's how seriously he's taking the curse, then he deserved to lose her!"

Curse? Key? My brows furrow in confusion as the witches banter back and forth. What the hell are they talking about? I shift, but the sound immediately draws their attention back to me. Their lips curl upwards into cruel grins as they take in my frightened expression.

"Look, the poor dear is scared," the first one says in a high-pitched, mocking tone.

I purse my lips, anger flaring within me. "Who are you? What do you want from me?" I can't keep my voice from quivering.

"Nakarr," the first one says. "Because when I suckled at my mother's teat, I drank the blood as greedily as I did the milk."

"Tegmine," the second one says. "Because Sadal Melik himself came to me under the full moon and gave me this scar." She lifts her forearm to display a jagged mess of flesh at the bottom of her elbow.

"He did not," Nakarr snaps, glowering at Tegmine.

My lips part in confusion and fear as they bicker. I don't know where I am or who these women are, but I'm more frightened than I was before. Their names are dark and menacing, as equally disturbing as their explanations.

"How dare you take the Ancient One in your name," Nakarr snarls.

Tegmine slaps her, the sound echoing through the cave. I flinch back, eyes wide with fear. "We must not speak of him anymore," she hisses.

They fall silent before Nakarr turns to me, "We haven't asked our Sister's name."

Sister? I shake my head, pressing myself even further into the cold wall. "You must have me confused with someone else, I don't know you. I have no sisters, I'm an only child."

"Not that kind of Sister," Tegmine purrs. "The true Sister, born of blood that has taken the same oath we have. The oath of the Bloodbane witches. The oath to serve the Ancient One."

Bloodbane witches? I had heard Acubens mention them to Navi before, they're enemies. "I'm human," I say.

Nakarr shakes her head. "The oath is strong in your blood."

"That's impossible," I mumble. "I have a human mother and a human father. I've never met a witch before, besides the occasional Wiccan."

"What is this Wiccan?" Tegmine asks. "Enemies of the Bloodbane?"

"They don't even know the Bloodbane," I say hurriedly, hoping I haven't just doomed any Wiccan that happens to stumble across a Bloodbane witch. "My point is I can't be your Sister."

Tegmine rushes towards me and I feel my heart skip a beat at the sight. She snatches my forearm and grips it tightly, her sharp nails pricking my skin. "Do you feel that?"

I begin to shake my head furiously but stop. I can feel my blood thrumming. It's like I can feel every single drop of it in my veins rushing through me. A sensitivity to my own life force I've never felt before. My heart pumps faster, nerves coiling my stomach. I don't want it to be true. "What is that?" I murmur.

Temine smiles and releases my arm. "That is the oath."

"How?" I breathe.

The two women exchange a dark glance. "That will be for Maaz to tell you. If she lets you live."

"If she lets me live?" I echo in disbelief. "What am I doing here? Why did you take me in the first place?"

Tegmine scowls. "We cannot let the Fae king have anyone of the Bloodbane witches."

"Why not?" My brows furrow in confusion.

"Only one with the oath in her blood can break the curse Maaz put on him," Nakarr says, her lips pulled into a smirk. "But no Bloodbane witch would betray her Sisters, not for some Fae king."

"What curse? Why would Maaz put a curse on him?" This is the first I've heard of Maaz, though I suspect she leads the Bloodbane witches.

"Altair refused Maaz many years ago." Nakarr shakes her head. "The stupid Fae thought she was below him."

Tegmine cackles. "His pride is now his doom."

I open my mouth to question them further when suddenly there's a deep rumbling from the front of the cave. Tegmine rises and slips a dagger from her belt. She stalks towards the entrance of the cave warily.

"Get up," Nakarr hisses. She wrenches me to my feet, and I feel that thrumming in my veins again.

Tegmine steps into the sunlight. Suddenly, a clawed paw bulldozes into her, sending her flying. She screams, and Nakarr shouts for her. I watch as Tegmine whirls on her attacker as it steps into view. A giant black panther with the wings of crows. Acubens.

"Nakarr!" Tegmine shouts.

Nakarr tosses me to the ground, I land with a sharp cry. "Stay put," she snaps, plunging towards Acubens.

I haul myself up, using the wall for support and stumble after her. The two witches dance around Acubens as he swats at them with his massive paws and snaps his teeth at them. My ears are ringing from hitting my head against the wall after Nakarr forced me back down. I don't know if going back to Altair is a good choice, based on what the witches have told me.

But what I do know is Maaz might kill me. And her temper is volatile enough to put a curse on a man who rejected her. I'm not sure I would be safer with her than with Altair. After all, he hasn't hurt me yet.

At the entrance of the cave, I watch as Acubens' teeth close around Nakarr's arm. She shrieks in pain and drives her blade towards him. Tegmine, on his other side, has her own blade plummeting towards him. I scream, loud enough that birds erupt from the trees and scatter across the sky. Acubens drops Nakarr's arm in time to dodge her blow, but Tegmine manages to drive her long dagger into his ribs.

He stumbles, hissing, and knocks her away with his sheer weight. She falls to the ground a yard away, struggling to rise. Nakarr cradles her arm, blood pouring over her fingers. Acubens turns to me, his face twisted in pain. "Get on," he commands.

I run towards him and clamber on top of his back, nestled just above his wings. With a roar, he beats his wings and lifts us off of the ground. Below us, Tegmine swipes at him, and I hear him grunt as her sword swipes against his exposed belly.

But then we're too high for them to strike us. I watch as the two Bloodbane witches retreat into the cave, trailing blood behind them. Acubens is silent, the only sound is the constant beating of his wings and the drum of his heart. I tangle my fingers in his fur, nausea welling within me as I realize just how high off the ground we really are.

"Acubens," I mumble. "It's too high."

"Shut up," he snaps. But he descends low enough that we're skimming the tree line.

I breathe a sigh of relief and lean over him. His fur is soft and his body is warm. It helps against the wind chill. "Thank you," I say, clutching him tighter.

He doesn't respond. We ride in silence together as I consider what the witches told me. I don't know what it means to be a Bloodbane witch, but I can't deny that I felt something inside me. Some power that I don't know how to tap into yet. I don't know if I want to though. Not if it makes me like them. Hard and cruel and wicked.

The steady beating of Acubens' wings falters and we drop sharply before he catches us again. "Acubens?" My brows twitch together with concern and fear.

"Almost there," he murmurs, his voice laced with pain.

I can see the castle rearing up before us, details slowly coming into view. I feel a sense of relief at the sight of it. The sun is setting, casting an orange glow over the facade. When I'm in the castle grounds, the stones look dark and the structure is menacing. But here, soaring towards it, I can see the delicate turrets and the detailed spires. It's right out of a fairy tale.

Acubens lurches as we pass over the wall. I can hear worried shouting below us, I see Navi and some of her soldiers waiting along the road. We drift over them unsteadily, descending lower and lower. I resist the urge to clench my eyes shut as the ground soars closer. Acubens' paws stumble as we land, running to a stop. His wings sag against the ground and he pants heavily.

When we've stopped, I slip off of him, trying to maneuver with my long skirts. Acubens slumps to the ground, groaning in pain. And then I see the blood coating his belly and his ribs, matting his fur. My eyes widen at the sight of it. His hazel eyes are on me, his mouth slack. I bite my lip, brows furrowed as I meet his gaze.

Suddenly, Navi pushes past me, shoving me roughly aside. I catch myself and watch as she calls for healers. Soldiers and servants crowd around Acubens, a few run off in search of healers. Navi rests a hand on Acubens side and whispers to him so softly I can't catch her words. But they seem to bring Acubens some comfort. He closes his eyes and his breath steadies.

The healer pushes through the crowd just as the last rays of the sun disappear behind the mountains in the distance. Caught in the dusky light of the evening, I watch in shock as Acubens' wings curl back into his body and as his frame shrinks to the size of a man's. His fur disappears, replaced with riding leathers and boots and normal skin. His face morphs slowly, the ears slimming and lengthening to Fae ears.

The servant's light torches for the healers to work by. My jaw is slack, eyes wide, as I stare down at Altair. Blood seeps from the wounds in his belly and side. The only remaining indication that Acubens and Altair are one and the same.

CHAPTER 9

ALTAIR

The first thing I notice is the pain. A sharp sting in my side and in my belly, like a burn. Then I notice the light against my eyelids. But it's not daylight, it's candlelight. I open my eyes slowly, letting them adjust to the light.

I see the green embroidered fabric of my canopy above me. So, I'm in my room. The last thing I remember is landing in the courtyard with Verity. Verity. I sit up, eyes wild. Pain lances through my body, and I hiss, clenching my eyes shut. The Fae heal faster than mortals, and even witches, but the wound is still fresh.

I ease back down, wincing as my abdomen straightens again. "That's not a very kingly look," Verity says. I turn, a little startled to see her seated at my bedside. She studies my face, her blue eyes dancing over my features. "But I suppose it's more kingly than a jaguar."

"What are you talking about?" I rasp, narrowing my eyes at her. By the codes of the curse, I can't affirm anything she has to say about the curse until she says it directly.

She cocks her head at me. "I know you turn into a beast during the day. I know you're Acubens. And I know it's a curse."

Relief floods through me. She knows. I've wanted to tell her since I first spoke to her the morning she regained consciousness. I only wish I could tell her more. But if I speak anymore of the curse, we'll have no hope of changing it. I can only believe that Verity is clever enough to realize why I've brought her here.

I start in surprise as her cool hand slips into mine. She laces her fingers through mine, holding me loosely. I look at her curiously, but she's staring down at our entwined hands. "You must think you're so clever," she murmurs.

"What?" I ask.

She turns her fierce eyes on me. "You must think you're so clever for tricking me into believing that you and Acubens are different. And that I might have an ally in him."

I give her a crooked grin. "Only because I knew you intended to use him against me."

"What him?" She scoffs. "I don't like being tricked."

"Neither do I," I quip.

Verity is so obstinate. Even in the face of her own actions, she insists on painting me as the villain. It's almost charming. Her blue eyes glimmer in the candlelight as she studies me with interest. She's never looked at me this long before. Usually, she looks away, insisting on ignoring me. Her tongue wets her lips as her eyes fall upon my face and I feel a surge of desire flood through me.

"Thank you," she says softly.

I lean closer to her, ignoring the pain that shoots through me. I grin slyly. "What was that?"

She rolls her eyes, but I see a smile teasing her lips. "Thank you," she says louder.

"You're welcome," I say, dipping my chin to her.

"So, what's going on with these mysterious Bloodbane witches?" She asks, propping her chin in her free hand. "Are they Fae?"

I narrow my eyes at her. "Do they look like Fae?"

"Don't be so sensitive," she says, but I see amusement in her eyes.

"Now who thinks they're clever?" I ask, cocking a brow at her.

"It's my revenge," she says. "These witches… why do they hate the Fae?"

"Besides the obvious fact that we're much better looking, I can't say," I muse.

Verity rolls her eyes. "I had no idea you were so vain."

"I've been waiting to surprise you, to show you that there are some downfalls to my charming personality," I say.

"So charming," she agrees, squeezing my hand a little tighter. "Navi told me you would recover quickly."

I nod. "The Fae heal quickly, much faster than mortals. In two days, I won't even have a scar."

"That's unbelievable," she murmurs. "What else makes the Fae different?"

"Longevity, some magic, speed, strength," I say blandly.

"Jealous," she sighs. "My father almost died you know. And the process they used to cure him almost killed him as well."

My lips part in surprise at her words. Verity and I haven't spoken of anything personal, not even when she confided in Acubens. My heart falls at her words. Mortals are so fragile. "I'm sorry," I say softly.

She shrugs her shoulders, but I can see the sorrow in her eyes. "He's alright now."

"What sort of man is he, your father?" I ask. I don't want her to leave just yet. I want her to stay and tell me everything about her. She's been on my mind since I brought her to my castle. And while she infuriates me to some degree, I feel an undeniable pull towards her.

"He's smart and kind. But he's goofy. When I was a girl, he used to pretend to find a coin behind my ear, and then he would give it to me so I could buy ice cream from the ice cream truck." She smiles, reminiscing.

"He sounds like a great man," I say. "I would love to meet him one day."

Verity laughs, like a bell chiming. "You wouldn't. He would try to tug your ears off."

I grimace. Fae ears are extremely sensitive. "That wouldn't be pleasant."

She grins and reaches up towards my ears. I snatch her wrist when she's inches from the tip of my ear. She gasps in surprise and her cheeks color. I release her, dropping my gaze. "I'm sorry. Fae don't like having our ears touched except under certain circumstances," I explain. "I hope I didn't hurt your wrist."

Verity's hair bounces softly around her shoulders as she shakes her head. I realize that she's wearing the same gown she wore the night she was kidnapped. Happiness and satisfaction blooms in my chest as I realize that she came directly to my room after we returned.

"You just surprised me," she says, curious eyes flitting to my ears again.

"I'm sorry," I apologize again.

She smiles mischievously. "You know that's the second time you've apologized to me. I'm starting to think your coldness is a facade."

I paste a look of disinterest on my face. "A momentary lapse."

"I should go now, let you get your rest," Verity chuckles.

My face falls as she releases her grip on my hand and stands. Her dress is covered in dust and the fine silk is torn in several places. She gives me a hesitant smile, as if she isn't sure what to do. We've never spoken this long before. And we've certainly never spoken this long without arguing. It's been unexpectedly pleasant, and I'm sorry to see her go. I want her to stay and show me all the different sides of her. I want her to stay and tell me about her family. And I want her to stay and hold me.

My hand snakes towards her and I grab hold of her wrist again. Her eyes dart towards my face in confusion. I tug her towards me, she loses her balance and falls onto my chest. I ignore the pain from the sudden pressure and wrap my arms around her. My lips find hers as my eyes slipped closed.

I kiss her deeply, my lips moving against hers. Desire and passion course through me as she kisses me back. I nip at her bottom lip, my teeth grazing the sensitive flesh there and I feel her body tremble. She moans softly, and the sound sets my blood racing.

I was frightened when I realized she had been taken. Not only because without her, I don't stand a chance of breaking this curse, but because I worried for her wellbeing. Bloodbane witches can be finnicky and impulsive. They were as likely to treat her well as they were to torture her.

She relaxes against me, letting my tongue slip into her mouth teasingly. She groans again, and I can feel the stiffness of her nipples through the thin silk of her gown. My hands rove over her back as I hold her.

Suddenly, she pulls away, her eyes wide with shock. She straightens and slaps a hand over her swollen lips, staring at me. "Verity," I say, reaching for her again.

She blinks at the sound of her name and then drops her hand from her lips. She narrows her eyes at me as the shock fades. And then she slaps me, a stinging blow to my cheek. I lift a hand to cup the smarting cheek as her eyes widen at the realization of what she's done. I choke down a laugh at her expression and lift a hand.

"Verity," I say, suppressing a smile.

But she spins on her heel and runs from the room. The door slams shut behind her, but I know Navi is on the other side. I know she likely heard everything and knows what happened between me and Verity. I drop my head back onto my pillow, grinning.

I don't know what came over me. Verity is a beautiful woman to be sure, but she still wants to return home. She doesn't want to be here with me. I think back to her ruined dress and the fact that she stayed by my side all this time. My heart pounds loudly as I think of it. I haven't felt interested in anyone in many years, decades maybe.

I would occasionally delight in the company of women, but it meant nothing. And I always left them feeling nothing. But with Verity, my heart is beating wildly, and my blood is rushing like fire through my veins. She's stubborn and clever. Funny and sweet. And beautiful of course. She's not afraid to slap a king who's gotten out of hand either.

My grin widens. That's exactly what I need. A woman who isn't afraid.

CHAPTER 10

Verity

I can't forget the sensation of Altair's lips against mine. Soft yet commanding. A shiver trails down my spine at the memory. Even now, a day later, I haven't been able to keep my mind off of it. Or deny that I desperately want another.

I haven't visited him since I left him last night. It's daylight now, so he won't be himself. I feel a sympathetic pain in my chest at the thought of the curse. To be trapped between two bodies, two selves, must be torture for him. I lift my eyes from the ground in surprise. I haven't doubted once what the Bloodbane witches told me. The longer I'm here, the more I come to believe that this is all real. It's no game or fantasy devised by a kidnapper.

Pursing my lips, I rise from the chair in my room and pace. If it is real, and I'm not trapped in my own hallucinations, then Altair truly does need my help. The witches told me I was Bloodbane. I don't know what that means, but the word itself sends my blood stirring. My brows furrow, confusion mingling with fear. Is my mother truly my mother? Or my father? Is my life a lie? I clench my hands into fists at my side, so tight that my knuckles are white. Who am I?

A part of me wishes Acubens—Altair—didn't rescue me from Nakarr and Tegmine, if only so I could meet this Maaz and learn my history from her. I chew my lip, trying to imagine what Maaz is like. She cursed Altair long ago, almost a thousand years. And yet, somehow, she's still alive. I imagine she's an old hag now, bent over with a hump on her back and long, scraggly gray hair.

Remarkably similar to cartoon witches in every children's movie.

Suddenly, a knock sounds at my door. I recognize the sharp, business-like raps of Navi. I open the door wide for her to enter. She looks me over coldly, hands clasped behind her back. I meet her gaze evenly. I get the sense Navi doesn't like me much.

"Yes, Navi?" I ask, looking at her expectantly.

"What did the Bloodbane witches want with you?" She asks.

I shrug. "They wanted to bring me to Maaz, I don't know why."

"What else did they tell you?" Her voice is laced with suspicion.

"Why do you want to know? I haven't done anything," I say, arching a brow.

"The Bloodbane witches came to our front door, killed two of my men, and snatched you. I want to know what they wanted with you," Navi snaps. Her eyes flash furiously, and I feel a tendril of fear in my gut. "It is my duty to protect Altair. He almost died for you. Surely you wouldn't be so callous as to deny me of information that could protect him from his enemies."

I drop into an arm chair and stare at the stone floor. "Your duty," I muse. "Are you in love with him, Navi?"

"How dare you." Her voice is cold.

I know instantly that I've crossed a line. And I don't know what possessed me to ask about her feelings for Altair in the first place. But every time she says his name, I feel my heart clench painfully. I purse my lips, considering her words and her anger. She has every right to her fury.

"The witches told me I was one of them. They said Altair needed me to break the curse but that a Bloodbane would never betray her Sisters," I say. "That's all that they told me."

Her eyes narrow at me. "And will you betray them? Or will you become the Bloodbane you are?" She spits.

I round on her, anger flaring within me. "I'm not sure if your disgust for me stems from the fact that I'm a Bloodbane witch or if it's because you can't help Altair the way I can, but you don't know me, Navi," I murmur. "I have no allegiance to the Bloodbane witches, just as I have no allegiance to you. I'll do what I want."

Wordlessly, Navi spins on her heel and stalks from the room. She moves lithely, like a predator. I know if she wanted to, she could cut me in two with one swipe of her blade. I sit back, fuming. I don't know why I said what I did, or why I asked her about her feelings for Altair. It truly is none of my business. But then why did I feel a spark of jealousy in my heart when she spoke of her duty to him? And why do I hate it when his name falls from her lips?

I dig my fingernails into the armrests and bite the inside of my cheek until I taste blood. I have no intention of returning to the Bloodbane witches. Blood doesn't make you family. And I'm not eager to meet the woman who cursed a man for a thousand years because he rejected her. Altair has let me live in a guest in his house, even though it always felt like a prison. I understand now why he never let me leave. He couldn't risk losing me if I could potentially save him.

If I could, I would break the curse. But I was raised in the mortal world. A world without magic or fairytale creatures like the Fae. I don't know anything about curses or spells. I lick my lips. I'll simply have to educate myself.

I rise and slip out of my room into the hall. Altair has two Fae soldiers stationed outside my room at all hours of the day. One breaks away from his post to follow me down the hall at a distance. I roll my eyes. I doubt the Bloodbane could get to me within the palace. Or perhaps Altair still suspects I'll run away. I press my lips into a thin line at the thought.

The palace is a sprawling complex of wings and halls and massive staircases. I didn't notice its beauty before when I was too angry and frustrated to take any notice of my surroundings beyond the nearest exits. The walls and floors are a light stone, the floors carpeted in red. Vases of fresh flowers line the halls, placed beside large windows that overlook the palace gardens and exterior buildings.

There's so much to this place that I haven't explored yet. I hadn't even realized the castle grounds were so large. But as I gaze out the windows, I realize I was only in a single piece of its gardens. I turn away from the windows towards a massive door-way. The library.

As I enter, my breath slips away from me in surprise. The library is two stories tall, filled with rows and rows of dark oak bookcases. Shelves line the walls from the floor to the ceiling, wooden ladders attached to each shelf so readers can reach the tomes on the highest shelves. Comfortable chairs dot the room, tucked away in corners and beside the few fireplaces I can spot along the walls. On the far wall, floor to ceiling windows let in masses of natural light. It's the most beautiful place I've ever seen. It would put any library in the world to shame, I think as envy tugs at my heart. It's been my dream since I was young to have a library like this.

Elated, I rush inside, smiling giddily. The soldier who trailed me here positions himself beside the entrance. I hurry to a nearby shelf and run my fingers over the leather-bound spines. They're warm to the touch, as if they've just been just put away.

"Can I help you?" A hoarse voice croaks behind me.

I gasp, a little startled, and whirl around towards the voice. An old woman stands before me, not a woman—a Fae woman. She eyes me, an amused glint in her eyes. "Are you the librarian?" I ask, taking in the deep wrinkles around her eyes and mouth.

"I am." She dips her chin. "You must be the Bloodbane."

I clench my jaw. "I'm a librarian as well."

"Are you?" She chuckles. "Then I don't suppose you'll need any help from an old Fae like me."

"Actually," I blurt, reaching a hand towards her. "I'm looking for anything you may have about curses or Bloodbane witches. I wouldn't know where to start in a library this size."

She arches a brow, lips pulled into a frown. "We don't keep tomes on Bloodbane magic here."

"Anything you have could be helpful to me," I say.

"Follow me," she says after a moment of silence.

She strides away, moving surprisingly fast for someone of her age. All the Fae I've seen in the palace have had youthful features, none appeared more than forty-years-old. Altair looks to be in his late twenties, and I know he's at least a thousand years old. This Fae woman must be ancient. She pulls me from my thoughts when she stops in front of a bookshelf tucked in the far corner of the library.

She taps on a book's spine and turns to me. "Start here. You may find what you need in this shelf."

"Thank you." I smile gratefully and start reading the titles of the books as she leaves.

"Just be careful," she calls. Her gray eyes gleam. "The oath might call too strongly."

I furrow my brows. "What do you mean?"

But there's no answer, and the woman is nowhere to be seen. I narrow my eyes towards where I last saw her, a sense of apprehension twisting inside me. It's probably nothing. The Fae are light-footed and graceful, like cats. I'm sure she simply slipped away before I could notice.

My spine tingles as I turn back to the tomes. *A History of the Fae, Third and Fourth Dynasties. Greater Religions of Alnembra.*

Curses and Spellwork, a Manual. I carry a load of thick books back towards the main area, where it's lighter. I pull the first book off the stack and open it on a reading table as I tuck myself into a padded chair.

Granuil Thoran of House Thoran of the First Dynasty became the first Fae to dabble in Bloodbane magic in the year 1023. Granuil pioneered modern Fae medicine through the invention of poultices and potions that aided in the healing process. A record of these potions is listed in the Index AB. Unfortunately, Granuil died in the first Civil War between the First and Second Dynasties before passing on his more detailed and complex work.

Eliza Thoran of House Thoran of the Second Dynasty continued his research and became known for her complex spells. Eliza spent much of her work studying the practice of reanimation, of which she was never successful. Eliza's failures in reanimation became helpful contributions to curse-breaking and protective spells. A list of these spells is listed in Index AC.

AC… AC… Hurriedly, I flip towards the back of the ancient book and scan over the different indexes. Finding it, I study the list intently, hoping that the names of the spells won't be too complex for me to guess their meaning. Finally, my finger rests over a single spell, one that sounds promising; oath-breaker.

I follow the footnote to another page, where more information on oath-breaker is written. I read, taking a few mental notes. Excitement and hope well within me as I read the instructions. This, I can at least try. Somehow, someway, I have Bloodbane magic in my veins. Perhaps I can use it to cast a spell to save Altair.

I bookmark the page and tuck it beneath my arm, heading to the soldier at the door. "I need chalk," I say.

His eyes drop to the book in my arms and then rise to meet my eyes. "We don't practice magic around here."

I purse my lips. "You might not. I'm trying to save your King."

The soldier stares me down before finally relenting. "I'll bring you chalk. But don't do that here."

"I won't. Bring it my room, please," I say as I sweep past him into the hall.

I practically run up the stairs and down the long halls, clutching the book tightly to my chest. In my room, I toss the book onto my bed and push the armchairs out of the way. Grunting, I move them back against the wall. Then, I roll up the ornate carpet on my floor and drag it beside the arm chairs. I need room, an open space.

As I'm laying the book out before me and flipping to the correct page, the door opens. The soldier enters and tosses me a stick of chalk. I catch it easily. Before I can thank him, he's shut the door. I wrinkle my nose at his abrupt departure. The Fae are magical creatures, and yet they abhor spells. If I visit Altair tonight, I'll ask him about it. I almost laugh at myself then. There is no 'maybe'. I want to see him.

Shaking my head to clear my thoughts, I start etching the spell on the floor with the chalk. I draw a large circle, uneven, but still a circle. In it, I copy the strange markings in the book; slashes of chalk that look almost like Viking runes. By the time I'm finished mapping it out, my trousers are dusted in white powder. I rise, surveying my handiwork.

It isn't a spell yet though. I move to the fire and carefully extract a bit of burning wood from it with the stoker. I hold it gingerly, the heat of the wood singing my fingers. With a sigh of relief, I drop the burning wood into my circle of chalk. Instantly, the chalk ignites into my flames. Sparks course through it like wildfire. It burns too hot too quickly and I lurch backwards, away from the smoke curling away from the spell.

As the sparks die out and all that's left is blackened ash, my blood thrums powerfully. I feel it rushing through me, every molecule, every bit of oxygen being carried by my cells. It's the same sensation I felt when the Bloodbane witches touched me, but a thousand times more powerful. My head swims and I stumble backwards into the arm chairs.

I lean heavily against them, breathing raggedly. What is happening? I feel the blood drain from my face as my body breaks into a cold sweat. My hands tremble uncontrollably. I clench my eyes shut and lower myself to the floor, struggling to catch my breath.

Slowly, gradually, the pain and nausea ease and the strength of my blood fades. I open my eyes. The ash covered chalk has faded to gray, cool now. Out the window, the sun is setting. I clutch at my head. How long was I lost? When I first started the spell, it was barely the afternoon. I've missed hours of the day. Fear coils in my heart, sending a wave of ice through my body. I don't know what's happening to me. But it scares me that I may not be who I thought I was.

I haul myself to my feet, taking a moment to make sure I'm steady. I don't want this spell to remain here. I don't want to look at it anymore. There's a small broom besides the fire, used to clean up any ashes that may have drifted away from the fireplace. I grab it and brush away the ash and chalk. I sweep the remnants of the spell into the fire, letting it burn away the evidence.

I wonder if I reacted that way because I was successful. I wonder if Altair is saved. My energy is slowly returning, and with it my curiosity. I return my room to normal before running out the door towards his room.

My heart is pounding loudly as I approach his door. The spell should have had immediate effects, but maybe he was too injured to come find me when it worked. Navi eyes me from her post at his door but I ignore her. I throw the door open and run breathlessly into the room. My heart soars when I see Altair. He's still lying in his bed, in the same position he lay in the night before. But his eyes are closed, and his lips softly parted. He's asleep. And he's Fae.

I bite my lip, trying unsuccessfully to force back a victorious grin. A soft breeze rustles the curtains at his balcony, and moonlight streaks into the room. Moonlight. My smile fades. It's night now. The curse is only doing what it always has done; freeing him when the sun sets. The spell failed.

Quietly, so as not to wake him, I curl into the chair at his bedside. I rest my head on my knees, rolling it back and forth so my knees almost massage my temples. I don't want to try another spell. Not after the effects the last had on me. It was painful and sickly and uncomfortable. And I didn't like trying to be someone I'm not. I'm not a Bloodbane witch, even if my blood does sing in response to magic. I don't want to be one.

I sigh softly, exhaling until my lungs are screaming for more air. If this were a story, the answer would be much simpler. Like a kiss for a frog to turn him into a prince. I lift my head and stare at him. Altair is handsome in the same way nightshade is beautiful. Tempting, but dangerous. I know he could take me anytime he wanted, force himself on me. But he hasn't yet. Except for the kiss last night, which hardly counts because I wanted it. I wanted it badly.

I press my lips together, thinking. Clearly, I'm out of my depth. I'm a librarian, not a curse-breaker. My best course of action would be to do more research. It was foolish of me to throw myself into a spell that I knew next to nothing about. I'm lucky nothing terrible happened.

I unravel myself and stand over him. I'll return to the library then, perhaps I'll find the old Fae woman and she can help me. Altair stirs in his sleep and takes a deep breath before settling. My eyes linger on his lips. It couldn't hurt to try the old-fashioned way to break curses. I'm out of ideas right now, anyway.

My heart is in my throat as I lean over him. I breathe him in; he smells like pine and fresh rain. Slowly, I lower my lips to his. Heat flushes through me as our lips meet. I hold my lips against his, they're soft and full. I curl my fingers into the mattress so I don't run them over his chest. If he would only wake up, I know I would let him take things further than a simple kiss.

My eyes snap open as the thought crosses my mind and I jump away. He hasn't moved and his breathing hasn't changed. Blushing, I run from his room and close the door softly behind me. I can't let myself get wrapped up in a simple kiss like that. It was to break the curse.

But my body responded to him in a way that it's never responded to Henry. I felt like a wave crashing to Altair's shore. Just like last night. I shake my head, wandering the halls to clear my mind. I'm here to break the curse, and nothing more. I have work to do.

CHAPTER 11

Altair

I open my eyes as the door clicks softly closed and Verity's footsteps echo down the halls. My heart is pounding wildly in my chest, blood roaring in my ears. I can still feel the soft press of her lips to mine, like a phantom kiss. It tingles.

I lift my fingers to my lips and touch them, wondering if it was real or just a dream. But I was completely awake, resting, when she entered. It made my heart soar when she sat beside my bed and didn't disturb me; as if she simply wanted to be in my presence. To be close to me the way I have started to crave being close to her.

And then the kiss. I felt her hovering over me, smelled the anxiety on her skin. And the desire. I run my tongue over my lips, tasting her. Groaning, I drag a hand over my jaw. I thought that Verity despised me, but now I wonder if it's all a show. A way for her to fight against her own desires.

A well of hope and happiness bubbles in my chest. If she could be falling for me little by little, the curse could be broken after all. The door opens and I glance towards it nervously, but it's only

Navi. She closes the door behind her and stands by my bedside, looking grim.

"What is it, Navi?" I ask, struggling to sit up.

"Don't, just rest," she says. She places her hands on my shoulders and gently pushes me back down on the bed.

"It feels strange talking to you when I'm lying down like this," I say.

She stares at the chair by my bedside. "But not when the mortal does."

I cock a brow. "She isn't my Captain of the Guard."

"Ah." She smiles stiffly. "When the mortal left, she seemed troubled, I wondered if anything happened between the two of you."

"Verity," I say.

"What?" She meets my eyes, looking startled.

"Her name is Verity," I say. "And no, I'm alright."

Navi purses her lips but quickly schools her face. I don't miss the flash of irritation in her eyes. "Good."

"I plan to hold a ball," I announce, a smile stretching across my face.

She looks up sharply. "Altair, I don't think that's wise. The mort- Verity was just abducted. Maaz knows she's here. We'll be vulnerable."

"In a week. We will have the ball in a week," I say. "The first in almost a thousand years."

"Altair," Navi murmurs. "A celebration like that would simply risk too much."

"Navi, everything will be fine." I pat her hand. "You more than anyone else know how close to failure we've come. But with Verity here, I think we're making progress. You've stood by me through it all, don't give up when we're so close."

"Yes, Your Grace," she whispers, slowly dragging her hand out from beneath mine.

I narrow my eyes in confusion. Navi hasn't used titles with me for almost two hundred years. "Is it something else?"

"Would you like anything to eat? I can have the servants fetch some light food for you," she says, ignoring my question.

I don't press her further. If Navi wants to confide in me, she will. I've learned to be patient with her, just as she has learned to be patient with me. "Maybe a little."

Without another word, Navi sweeps out of the room, the candlelight glinting off the gold in her sheath. My brows knit together as the door closes behind her. Strong and stoic, Navi rarely shows emotions. She's the one I trust to be there when I fly into a rage. But something is bothering her, of that I'm certain. I need her to focus. With Maaz on our scent and aware of Verity's existence, I trust Navi more than anyone else to protect Verity.

When she returns with a broth soup, she doesn't stay, and I don't ask her to. Alone, I drink the soup greedily. I haven't eaten since the disastrous dinner with Fayne. As I drain the last drops of the soup and consider calling for another, the door creaks open.

I suppress a smile when Verity pokes her head into the room. Her brows are crumpled nervously, but when she catches my gaze, she plasters a look of confidence on her face. I stare stonily at her and set my bowl aside. It clatters loudly but she doesn't flinch at the noise.

"What do you want?" I ask, arching a brow as she closes the door behind her.

She strides towards me, dressed in a simple, form-fitting gown that perfectly accentuates her figure. I drag my eyes over her hips and breasts, pleased when I hear her breath hitching in her throat. Her skirts rustle as she settles into the chair at my bedside.

Verity holds up a book and waves it at me. "I'm here to read. I thought you might be bored," she says. She eyes me. "Was I wrong?"

"Quite." I toss her an arrogant grin. "I find my own company stimulating."

Her eyes dart to my groin before returning to meet my eyes. "I'm sure."

I chuckle. "Curious?"

"Not at all," she quips, standing. "I'll leave you to it then."

I watch as she stomps to the door, her hips sashaying attractively. When her fingers graze the doorknob, I call out to her, "Wait."

"What?" She twists, a soft blush creeping to her cheeks.

"Read to me." She raises her brows but doesn't move. I sigh. "Read to me *please*."

With a victorious smile, she returns to my side. She opens the book. "In the year 532 a great beast roamed the lands. He made his home in the mountains, deep in the dark caves and abandoned mines. He was the only one of his kind and felt very lonely."

"Is this a children's book?" I scoff.

"I thought it would be simple enough to hold your attention," she says, snickering.

"I think you'll find my attention can be focused for a very, very long time," I say, my voice low and soft.

She runs her tongue over her lips and then shifts in her seat and I know I've got her. "Then I'll read the real story. I found it in your library."

"Which one is it?" I crane my neck to read the title.

She angles it towards me. "*Runyun*."

"Ah." I lean back, smiling to myself. "One of my favorites."

"You've read it?" She asks, surprise lacing her voice.

"Verity, I've read every book in that damn library twice," I sigh. "What else would I do with a thousand years of stagnant existence?"

She frowns, brows furrowing. "I'm sorry. I wish I knew what to do, but I don't."

"Don't think of it." I wave a hand. "Please, read."

"In the days of the fiercest barbarians and tribesmen, there arose one stronger than all the rest. A young Fae boy named Runyun. He could crush a mountain troll's skull in one blow with his great hammer. Bloody a Fae warrior's head with one strike of his bare fist. He ruled over the clans and created their laws. Runyun was the most powerful Fae in all of Alnembra. He had everything. But he didn't have a woman…"

Verity's voice is soft and melodic as she reads the tale of Runyun. I close my eyes, letting the vision of Runyun's heroic search for a lover flit across my eyes. I was a boy when I first heard this story; told to me by my nursemaid. My father disapproved of such stories, but my mother loved them. And his heart belonged to her, so the tales continued. I sigh, forcing my thoughts to stray away from my dead parents and back to Verity.

As she reads, her voice grows softer and softer. Or maybe I'm just going farther and farther away. I drift off to sleep as she reads of his first encounter with the mortal maiden. And I dream of Verity.

CHAPTER 12

VERITY

I tug the waist of the ball gown, frowning at myself in the mirror. The strapless gown is made of teal satin, with heavy beads dotting the bodice and the full skirt. Fae maids laced me into it only moments before, after pinning my hair up in a complicated braid. I pick at one of the beads on the bodice, a large crystal, and wonder if it's real.

Altair had the gown made for me. He delivered it to my room himself this morning, when he told me that he was throwing a ball. I try to quell the excitement tingling in my chest. My own wedding would have been the closest thing to a real ball that I had ever gone to, but I never did make it. And this gown is more exquisite than my wedding dress. The color is rich, and the design is simple yet elegant. I never thought I would like a dress with such a heavy skirt, but with my waist cinched so tightly, it looks beautiful.

Altair is recovered now, just in time for the surprise ball. He healed quickly, but he told me he would. I'm still having a difficult time accepting the fact that he truly is Fae, a fairytale creature. But I've seen enough now that there's no denying he isn't human. I close my eyes and picture him, what he might look like when I join him in the ballroom. Those hazel eyes drinking me in as a pleased grin plays across his lips.

I open my eyes, breathing shallowly. My heart is beating quickly, heat blooming in my chest and cheeks. Altair has been on my mind too much lately. I think of him during the day as I study spells and potions, and I visit him at night. I've even slept in his room, in the chair beside his bed.

I bite my lip, smearing the lipstick. I can't do this. I'm engaged still. Even if I don't want to be. Even if I never loved Henry at all, I still couldn't allow myself even the slightest chance of betraying him. And these feelings, the attraction I feel for Altair, are very real. Very real and very tempting. I take a deep breath, trying to calm myself.

There's a soft knock at the door, and Navi enters. She's dressed in her typical clothes; trousers and a leather cuirass. But the cuirass is embroidered with golden threads. Despite her casual wear, she looks stunning. Her green eyes never shift from my face. Music and laughter float through the open door, the only indication of the ball.

"Are you ready?" She asks.

I nod. "What can I expect? I've never been to a Fae ball. Or a ball at all."

She leads me down the hall towards the main staircase, her boots clipping against the stone floor. "Members of Altair's court will be in attendance, treat them with respect. You may find resistance to your presence from some but ignore it."

"Resistance?" I frown. "Why?"

"You're mortal," she says simply.

I exhale sharply through my nose. "With thousands of years to contemplate existence I wouldn't have expected to find bigotry among the Fae."

"With thousands of years of watching you mortals destroy

yourselves and everything around you, you mean," Navi says, eyeing me.

"That's one way to look at it, I suppose." I narrow my eyes.

At the bottom of the stairs, she halts. I turn, brows furrowed with confusion. But she simply tilts her chin towards something behind me. "Verity." Altair's silky voice rings out behind me.

My cheeks heat at the sound. I can feel his presence behind me, as if the molecules between us are quaking. I face him and take him in. He's dressed in well-fitting trousers, tucked into shining leather boots. His jacket is buttoned completely, black and embroidered in gold threads. His black hair is combed back, coifed attractively, and he's shaved off the ghost of a beard he grew during his week of bedrest.

"You look lovely," he says, his voice a little hoarse.

I run my fingers along my skirts. "Thank you for the dress."

He holds a hand out, standing stiffly. "Shall we?"

I wrap my fingers around his and let him lead me to the grand doors of the ballroom. I take a deep breath, excitement and nerves sparking in my chest. "Navi told me not to embarrass you," I say.

"A well-intended request." He smirks. "But you'll find I'm not easily embarrassed."

The servants at the doors drag them open and then we're awash in golden light from the crystal chandelier in the center of the ceiling. The music fades softly and Altair steps forward, tugging me along with him. I bite my lip nervously as we enter the ballroom and suddenly hundreds of pairs of eyes are on us.

"Your King!" A servant beside the door bellows.

The rustling of skirts and jackets is thunderous as the Fae sweep into curtsies and bows. My eyes widen at the number of beautiful, lithe beings in the room. Dressed in gowns of rich hues and bright colors, all the Fae women could have graced the cover of Vogue. Altair leads me further into the room, I blanch inwardly as all of their eyes rake over me.

The Fae tower over my petite frame, their intelligent eyes glistening predatorily. I shrink closer to Altair instinctively and his hand slips away from mine to wrap around my waist. He bends low over my ear. "I hope you know how to dance," he breathes.

A pleasant shiver runs along my spine as his breath wafts over my ear and neck. "Right now?" I ask, my panicked eyes darting across the faces in the crowd.

"Right now," he confirms, spinning me towards him.

He takes my hand, sweeping me into his arms deftly. I catch myself before I stumble and try to relax into his grip. I took a few dancing lessons before the wedding. Henry wanted to dance properly during the reception, but I never practiced much. Now I'm wishing I had.

I swallow with some difficulty as the music swells. With a sly grin, Altair slides easily into the waltz, leading me gracefully across the dance floor. I hold my breath, focusing on keeping my feet moving in time with his. His eyes glitter as he watches me, lips twisted in amusement.

"You look as frightened as a rabbit," he murmurs.

"I feel like it." I grip his hand a little tighter, my knuckles whitening.

"You don't have to hold so tightly, I won't let you go," he says softly.

I look away from the crowd and meet his gaze. It's soft now, gentle even. My heart drums unsteadily in my chest. "I'm not a very good dancer."

After a moment his eyes take on the familiar cold, clever gleam. "It's disappointing really. You have the petite frame of a dancer."

"Imagine how I must feel," I mutter, too nervous to play his games.

"Get ready," he whispers.

I look at him, alarmed. "For what?"

Suddenly, as the music swells to its finale, Altair sends me into a far-reaching spin. He draws me back to him, and when I reach him, my back is pressed against his chest. We sway for an instant before he gives me a final twirl and dips me dramatically. My hands are slick with sweat, eyes filled with anger and fear. Altair's face hovers over my own, his hazel eyes darting between my eyes and lips.

He grins roguishly and pulls me back up. I scowl, but he tuts softly, reminding me that his court is watching. Furiously, I paste a smile on my face and curtsy as the onlookers applaud. Soon, the rest of the attendees file onto the dance floor as another waltz begins. I push away from Altair and stalk to the outskirts of the room to catch my breath.

I lean against a wide marble pillar, a beautiful earthy tone in the warm light of the ballroom. The opposite wall is lined with floor to ceiling windows, with elegant red velvet curtains draped over them. Flowers in tall vases line the room, and Fae carrying flutes of alcohol wander through the crowds. I close my eyes and wipe my palms on my skirts.

When I open them, I expect to find Altair in front of me, with a clever remark or an apology. But he isn't there. My brows twitch together as I scan the crowd. I see him on the dance floor, spinning a beautiful Fae woman in a rose blush gown. She makes eye contact with me and I bite my lip as I see her bright turquoise eyes.

Jealousy wells in my chest as I watch her head tilt back with laughter. Altair smiles and murmurs something else to her. I prick my fingers with the nail of my thumb and force myself to turn away. I don't understand what this feeling is.

The Fae pay no attention to me as I wander along the fringe of the crowd towards the refreshment tables. There's a fountain of wine on one and I watch curiously as a Fae man dips his goblet directly into it. I shrug and follow suit, filling my goblet to the brim. I need wine. A lot of wine.

I sip it slowly, trying to appear delicate and confident instead of the nervous wreck that I am. A man appears at my side, dressed in forest green. He bows sharply and then grins at me. "You must be the Key," he says.

"Verity," I say hesitantly, extending a hand.

He takes it and presses one of my knuckles to his lips. "A pleasure to meet you, Verity."

"I'm sorry, I don't know your name," I say, fishing. He's handsome, in a more angelic way than Altair.

"Thalamain." He smiles. "My friends call me Thal."

"Then I'll call you Thalamain until we become friends." I lift my cup, half-empty now.

His smile broadens. "Any friend of my cousin is a friend of mine."

"Your cousin?" I arch a brow.

"Altair," he says simply.

My lips quirk into a surprised smile. "Altair is your cousin? I can't imagine what it was like growing up with him."

He laughs loudly, drawing the attention of a few nearby Fae. "He's always been a little monstrous, believe it or not."

"I believe it," I murmur into my goblet.

"Do you?" Altair asks, his chest brushing against my shoulder. I grimace, meeting Thal's eyes. He grins at me, clearly enjoying the moment. "I see you've met my cousin."

"Altair, good to see you," Thal says, reaching for Altair.

They embrace, clapping each other on the back. "And you." Altair grins and ruffle Thal's long black hair. "You look like a rogue."

"What can I say, the women seem to find it charming," Thal says wickedly. He grows serious, gripping Altair's arm tightly. "It is good to see you, cousin. It's been too long."

Altair clenches his jaw, the muscle throbbing, and nods. "It has."

Thal turns to me, the grin returning to his face. "And I suppose we have this woman to thank for it."

"It's not every day abductees are thanked for their presence," I say, taking another sip of my wine.

Thal and Altair are silent, their brows arched in surprise. Altair's lips quirk into a smile just as Thal barks out a laugh. "Careful cousin, I may have to steal her from you. I like this one." His green eyes rake over me.

"Ignore him," Altair says, smiling. "He's a drunk fool."

"It's a special occasion." Thal lifts his glass. "My reclusive cousin has finally emerged into the public eye without the feathers."

"Verity, a dance?" Altair asks, shoving Thal aside playfully.

Thal chuckles and strides away towards a group of Fae women clustered together in the corner. I cock a brow as he bows charmingly. Altair follows my gaze and purses his lips. He plucks the wine from my hand and passes it off to a servant, ignoring my protests.

"If you like him so much why don't you drag him away from those women," Altair snaps.

I scoff and march towards the fountain to get another glass, but Altair stops me, his hand gripping my wrist. He tugs me towards him and into his arms. I squirm, trying to pull away bit his arms are tight around me.

"Verity," he says, his voice low, seductive.

I still, my heart pounding loudly in my chest. So loud I know he can hear it. The sound of my name slipping so smoothly from his lips has my skin on fire. "What?" I ask, though it doesn't sound as harsh as I intended.

"I," he begins before halting. He grinds his teeth in frustration, glowering. "Never mind."

"What?" I whisper, surprise lilting my voice as his arms fall away. I feel cold now.

He clears his throat. "Dance with me, please."

I narrow my eyes. "What happened to the blue-eyed Fae from before? You seemed quite taken with her. I'm sure she'll dance with you again."

"What woman?" His brows furrow and then recognition sparks in his eyes. "It's only polite that I dance with several woman throughout the night."

"Well then you should probably continue your rounds." I gesture broadly at his guests.

"Perhaps later," he says, and I recognize the stubborn edge to his voice. "But for now, I would like to dance with you."

My heart flutters in my chest at his words. "Fine."

"Don't sound so elated," he says teasingly, holding a hand out for me.

I take it, ignoring the way my blood sings when he wraps his fingers around mine. "I never pegged you for the type that needs your ego stroked," I say, following him through the crowd to the dance floor.

He places a warm hand on the small of my back and pushes me closer to him as we take to the floor. His hazel eyes are lit with some emotion I can't quite place, a smile tugging at his lips. "Even Kings have weaknesses. Perhaps you're mine."

My lips part in surprise at his words. "Oh."

"No witty remark?" He teases. "What a shock."

"Just give me a moment, I'm sure I'll think of something," I lie.

He chuckles. "I would wait all night."

"What are you doing?" I ask, looking him squarely in the eyes. "Why are you saying these things? And talking to me like this?"

"What are you talking about?" He sweeps us between two other couples.

"You're starting to sound like a romantic," I say.

Altair lowers his face and I almost close my eyes, expecting a kiss. But he presses his cheek to mine, his breath wafting over my ear pleasantly. "What should I sound like?"

I shudder and instinctively lean into him. But then he's

sending me into a twirl, grinning wickedly. I almost stumble on my blue skirts, but he catches me and steadies me in his arms as we continue sweeping over the dance floor.

"Never mind," I mutter, glowering at him.

Suddenly, the ballroom doors slam open and a chill gust of wind blows powerfully through the room. The music comes to a screeching halt, and the chatter dies down. Altair freezes, his hands on my shoulders protectively as he stares towards the ballroom doors. My hairs stand on end and a shiver trails down my spine. Like a spider crawling over my skin.

"Hello there, old friend," a woman's voice echoes over the crowd.

I yelp as Altair shoves me away from him into Navi's waiting arms. She must have appeared behind us while our attention was on the door. She drags me back into the crowd and away from Altair just as a woman in a blood red cloak saunters towards Altair. I don't struggle against her, knowing well enough that Altair would never dismiss me so roughly without good reason.

Navi stops beside one of the pillars, her sword drawn in her hand. Thal appears beside me, his green eyes locked onto the woman's confrontation with Altair. The woman is tall and lithe, just as graceful as the Fae. Her icy blonde hair is loose and long, hanging past her waist. And her pale blue eyes never move from Altair. Blue eyes like mine.

The woman unties her red cloak, revealing a sparkling silver gown beneath with a drastic neckline that reaches her navel. She sways towards Altair and he stiffens. The woman reaches him and rests a thin hand on his cheek, gesturing towards the crowd.

"You throw a party and don't invite me?" She croons. "How cold."

"Get out of here, Maaz," Altair growls.

Maaz. My jaw drops, eyes wide as I take in the witch that ruined Altair's life. The Fae surrounding them watch anxiously, fear glittering in their eyes. They're afraid of Maaz. I furrow my brows in confusion. How could an entire room of powerful Fae be frightened of a single Bloodbane? From the corner of my eye, I see Thal draw a dagger from his waist.

"Come, Altair, there's no need for such poor manners," Maaz pouts. "I'm a guest. Offer me refreshments."

He shakes free of her, slapping her hand away. "You're no guest. Now leave, before I cut you down."

She tuts like he's a disobedient child. "You always were stubborn, weren't you? It's one of the things I love about you."

"Get. Out," he says through gritted teeth.

Nausea hits me as she speaks, as she so casually mentions her love for him. Navi hisses, enraged.

"No wine then? No little desserts on those delicate papers you Fae love so much? No? None of that?" Maaz looks expectantly at Altair before shrugging. "Let's get down to business then."

"Speak." Altair glowers at her.

"Two little birdies told me you had the Key," Maaz says lightly. "I was so curious, I had to come see for myself. It only took you nine hundred and ninety-nine years. Now, where is she?"

I shrink back against the pillar and Navi steps defensively in front of me. Dread coils in my chest and I know that if Maaz finds me, she'll likely kill me. Altair steps towards her, crowding her and driving her back a step.

"Leave. By the accords of the curse I can't kill you, but I can torture you. And you've waltzed right in to my palace. Surrounded by my people," Altair says, his voice low and dangerous. "Get out."

"So testy," Maaz quips. "I'll go. But you keep an eye on your precious Key, darling. Because you're running out of time, and I'm only just getting started."

Maaz rakes her eyes over the crowd before settling on me. She grins sinisterly and draws up her hood. My heart stops for an instant when our eyes meet. We watch as she melts back into the crowd, and the doors creak shut behind her. The Fae in the ballroom collectively let out a sigh of relief when she's gone, and Navi sheaths her sword.

Altair is beside us in an instant. "Let's go, Verity."

"What?" I ask as he takes my hand, pulling me away from the pillar.

Behind us, the music never picks up again, and Fae mutter amongst themselves as they leave the ballroom. Maaz's presence has brought the celebration to a halt. Altair doesn't say goodbye to his guests before ushering me up the grand staircases towards my room. I hold my skirts high so I can keep up with him, his long legs carrying him quickly through the halls.

There are guards all around us, hurrying to different posts throughout the castle. Twice as many as there were before. Altair's back is stiff with anger, and I can feel it washing off of him in waves. He stops outside my door and I stare up at him, brows furrowed with concern.

I've never seen Altair this furious, or this afraid. I lay a hand on his arm, squeezing gently. He looks up, dragging his hand away from his eyes. "That was her," I say.

He nods stiffly. "It's too dangerous for you now that she knows you're here."

"I'm trying," I murmur. "And I won't wander away."

Altair presses his lips into a thin, anxious line. "I don't want to restrict you anymore than I already have, but please stay close. Please."

His pleading sends a pang of sorrow through my chest. "I will, I promise."

Our eyes meet, hazel and blue. And suddenly his lips are on mine, kissing me as if we'll never embrace again. I wrap my arms around his neck as our lips move together. He eases my lips apart with his tongue and I moan as he deepens the kiss. I nip at his bottom lip and he growls, pressing me closer to him. His arms around my waist, a hand on my ass. I arch into him, gasping as his fierce kisses drown me in desire.

I give into him and tangle my fingers in his hair. My body is on fire, lava trickling over me slowly. I've never wanted anyone this badly. Altair sucks my bottom lip, tugging on it, and I press myself against him in response. Waves of pleasure crash into me as he kisses me. My fingers graze the tips of his ears as I rake them through his hair and suddenly Altair is trembling violently. He groans and bites sensually on my lip.

His hands trail over my back, cupping my ass and pushing me against him. I gasp, clutching at him. No one has ever lit me on fire like this before, not even Henry. Henry. I freeze and push away from Altair, breathing heavily. Henry.

Panting, Altair adjusts his jacket and gives me a hesitant smile. "No slap?" He asks teasingly.

I bite my lip, staring into his beautiful hazel eyes. My words are lodged in my throat. The pleasure fades, but my desire for Altair is strong, tugging me towards him. But I can't. I'm still engaged.

CHAPTER 13

ALTAIR

Verity is warm in my arms, pliable and soft. She moans against my lips and the sound sends a thrill coursing through me. For the past week while I've been resting from my wounds, all I've been able to think about is Verity. When I'm not thinking of her, I'm obsessed with finding ways to keep her safe. Today's incursion from Maaz has only made it even clearer that verity can never be safe until she breaks my curse.

Her fingers tangle in my hair, drawing me from my thoughts and back to the woman in my arms. I take a ragged breath and sweep my tongue through her mouth, tasting her. A shock of pleasure hits me as her fingers gently trail the curve of my pointed ear. I shudder uncontrollably and a groan escapes my lips. Fae ears are intense erogenous zones, and Verity has stumbled upon it to my pleasure.

I need her desperately. A week of keeping my distance and quelling my attraction for her was annihilated tonight when I saw her in this gown. I squeeze her ass tightly, pushing her against my pelvis. She gasps softly and curls her body into me, as if she needs me as much as I need her. But she couldn't possible crave me to the same extent; every cell in my body is crying out for her.

Suddenly, she lurches away, panting. I drop my arms from around her, letting her create distance between us. My breath is coming in short, loud gasps as I reel from the kiss. It was heavenly being so close to her, being able to express how I truly feel for her. She stares up at me, eyes wide and impossibly blue. I offer her a smile, my heart soaring.

"No slap?" I tease.

She bites her lip and opens her mouth to speak before closing it hesitantly. I grow wary, watching her process the kiss. Her brows are furrowed and she's biting down her lip so hard I worry she may draw blood. I reach for her, my fingers skimming the soft skin of her arm. She shivers but doesn't relax the way I expected.

I frown. I may have pushed her too far, but I felt closer to her this last week than ever before. But perhaps the feelings between us haven't progressed as quickly as I thought. I smooth back my hair and drag a hand over my jaw.

"Goodnight, Verity," I say reluctantly.

I know she needs to rest; she's kept strange hours for me this past week. But I don't want to leave her tonight. A small corner of my heart desperately hopes that she'll invite me in, that she'll ask me to stay with her. But the inexplicable expression on her face tells me otherwise. Her forehead creases even deeper at my words, and she smooths her hands over her skirts nervously.

"What is it?" I ask, reaching for her.

She takes a smooth step back, her skirts rustling. "You shouldn't touch me," she murmurs.

A cold chill spreads through my chest and any shred of hope I had is torn. I realize as I stare into her sorrowful eyes that she isn't thinking of me at all. Her thoughts are on the mortal man she unwillingly left behind. The cold spreads from my heart to my limbs, an icy rage.

I turn, back stiff. I can't be with her while she thinks of him. Not after sharing such passion. Dawn isn't far off, and when it comes, I'll throw myself into the sky and patrol the borders to take my mind off of Verity. Though I know nothing could truly push her from my mind.

"Wait, Altair," she says. I feel her finger trips graze my back and I shudder.

"What?" I ask hoarsely.

"I need to see Henry, please, can I go?" Her voice is laced with nerves, as if she's afraid of what I might say. "I'll come back."

I chuckle humorlessly. "You want to see your mortal fiancé? Your lover?"

"I-," she begins, but I cut her off.

"Do whatever you want, Verity Chastain," I say coldly.

"Altair." She reaches for my elbow, but I glide to the side, just out of reach.

I look over my shoulder at her, my eyes dark and furious. "I don't care what you do."

Her eyes narrow. "You're being childish."

"Childish?" I arch a brow. "I thought you would be pleased; I'm releasing you to return to your lover and your family."

"It's your fault," she hisses. "I wouldn't ask to go back if it weren't for you."

I bristle, shoulders stiffening. "I'm so repulsive you simply can't stand my presence any longer? Then I'll free you." I turn and shout down the hall, "Navi!" fury lacing my voice.

She strides around the corner, her face carefully blank. "Yes, Altair?"

"Escort Verity to the nearest portal," I say, waving lazily towards Verity's irate figure.

Navi's lips part in surprise. "Altair, surely--"

"Now," I whisper forcefully. "Do it now."

"Come with me," Navi commands, turning to Verity. As they stride away, Navi's bright green eyes slip towards me.

I avoid Verity's gaze. She stares at me as she passes, but I gaze resolutely at the wall behind her. When they've disappeared around the corner, my shoulders sag in defeat. Verity still insisted on leaving, even after we grew closer. I laugh mirthlessly, what could I have expected, anyway? I brought her here against her will, befriending her doesn't change that.

I stalk to my room, anger boiling in my gut. Heat washes over me as I replay my time with Verity in my mind. Her initial obstinance. Her charm. The moments she told me of her family. Her lilting voice as she read to me each night. All of it meant nothing to her.

The walls shake as I slam the door behind me. I move to the balcony and peer over it, towards the cliff face below. At the bottom of this cliff is the nearest portal to the human world. I had my scholars create it nearby and within view of my room purposefully. I regret it now. I can't resist watching knowing that I have a clear view of the portal from my room.

I watch as Navi appears around the bottom of the cliff, Verity in tow. She's still dressed in her elegant gown. A dress I had specially commissioned for her, to match her eyes. A soft, blue light flares in the darkness below as Navi opens the portal. She gestures for Verity to enter. But Verity hesitates, her head tilting up towards me.

She may be able to make out my figure in the night, but her mortal eyes are too weak to see my expression, or the way my hands grip the railing so tightly my knuckles are white. I can see her face perfectly with my Fae eyes. I can see her forehead creased, with worry or regret or fear—I don't know. She runs her tongue over her lips, a nervous habit.

And then she's gone.

The portal flares once more before it closes. and I know Verity has made it safely to the mortal realm. Navi glances up and I can see the concern written clearly over her face. In her eyes, she just released the only woman who could save us from doom.

I clench my fists, imagining Verity reuniting with her lover. They'll make love and she might tell him about her experience. But she won't tell him everything. She won't tell him about the way she kissed me or that we need her. She'll conveniently leave out the little details. And we'll be gone by the time she forgets about us many years later.

The rage hits me like a boulder. I roar; a fearsome, sorrowful, and furious cry that echoes through the night. Birds burst from the trees below, disturbed from their nesting. I whirl away from the balcony and plunge into my room, striking anything within reach. I lash out at the mirror, shattering it completely. I catch my reflection in the shreds. A man with a face so twisted with anger and fear I don't recognize him.

Pain lances through my chest and I go still. I stand in the center of my room, torn apart, breathing raggedly. Verity is gone. It's likely she'll never return. How can I trust a mortal? How can I trust a woman with the Bloodbane oath in her veins? I close my eyes as the rage fades. It's my fault for trusting her. My fault for allowing her to get close to me.

She played me. Just as she intended from the beginning.

CHAPTER 14

Dawn in Times Square is the most peaceful time in the busy tourist and business district of New York City. The dirty cement of the sidewalk digs into my bare forearms as I try to catch my breath. The portal spit me out directly in Times Square, onto a thankfully empty sidewalk. The morning rush won't begin for another hour or so, despite the sun peaking over the city skyline.

I struggle to my feet; the mammoth skirt of my gown keeps getting stuck under my feet. I curse under my breath and manage to right myself. I dust off the grime of the sidewalk from my arms and hike the bodice of my dress up. The portal left me out of breath, sweating, and messy. My hair is sticking out every which way from the braid.

In the distance, I see a homeless man wandering my direction. Normally, I wouldn't be concerned. But it's early morning in New York and I'm dressed in a ball gown with genuine crystals. I need to get off the street.

I jog down the sidewalk, skirts in hand, towards a corner where I know I'll find a cab. All around me, buildings soar into the sky, bright neon lights shining through the murky light of dawn. Discarded cigarettes and chewing gum litter the ground. The owner of a corner grocery drifts out of his story and shakes his head at the fresh graffiti on the wall. Our eyes meet and he snorts.

The optimism of New Yorkers truly is undeniable. I roll my eyes.

At the corner, I raise a hand and wave it towards an oncoming cab. When he stops, I slide into the back seat, dragging my skirts behind me. My face peeks out of a massive wave of blue tulle. "350 Central Park West," I say, meeting the cab driver's gaze in the rearview mirror.

"Figures," he scoffs, peeling away from the curb. "You miss the limo?"

I smile sarcastically. "The horse and buggy, actually."

He barks out a laugh. "So, you doing the walk of shame or did the magic ball go all night?"

I sigh, nerves twisting in my stomach at the thought of meeting Henry after so much time. "Neither actually."

"Ah," the cab driver says knowingly. "There's a story here."

"You wouldn't believe it." I give him a strained smile.

Without the congestion of New York City traffic, we reach the curb of Central Park West in minutes. "Twenty dollars and thirty-three cents," he says, twisting around to face me.

"I don't have any money on me, but if you wait, I can bring some down," I say, blanching.

"Wait?" The driver sputters. His face turns an angry shade of purple. "Listen, here, I'm not waiting."

"Well you wait and get paid or you drive away, and you don't," I snap. I tear a large crystal from my dress and toss it to him.

He catches it. "What the hell is this?"

"Payment," I say, scooting out of the cab. "Take it to a jeweler."

The cab driver holds it up to the light and inspects the crystal. "How do I know it's real?"

"You don't. Here, have another." I throw him another large crystal and slam the door shut.

I hear him grumbling as he pulls away, but I know he'll get good money for those jewels. I turn to the entrance of Henry's swanky apartment complex; the doorman is watching me curiously. I smile as I approach, trying to smooth my hair. As I get closer, I see it's a doorman I've met before, Charles.

"Hi, Charles," I greet him hopefully.

His eyes are wide as he studies my face. "Miss Chastain?"

"Verity, please." I wave a hand. "Can you let me up? I need to see Henry."

"Miss—Verity, Henry is going to be thrilled to see you," Charles says hurriedly, breaking out into a smile. "Go on up."

"Thanks, Charles." I run through the door towards the elevators.

The closer I get to Henry's apartment, the more my gut twists. And the more Altair flickers through my mind. I close my eyes and rub my temples. He was furious when I asked to see Henry, as I knew he would be. But I couldn't bear to kiss him as if Henry had never existed. It would have been easier that way, but every time I feel that flicker of desire when I see Altair, it's always followed by guilt.

I pause outside Henry's door, my fist raised to knock. It's been weeks since I've seen him, weeks since our ruined wedding. And somehow, those weeks felt like an eternity. Finally, I drop my fist to his door and knock loudly. I hear him stirring within, his footsteps approaching. My hands tremble.

Henry opens the door, dressed in sweats and a t-shirt, a mug of coffee in hand. I smile tentatively at him. "Hello, Henry."

His jaw goes slack, eyes wide. "Verity?"

"Yeah," I say softly. "I'm back."

"Oh my god, Verity." He wraps an arm around me, dragging me into his chest. He crushes me to him, driving the air out of my lungs. I squeeze my eyes closed. When he releases me, he holds my hand tightly and drags me inside his apartment. "Come in, come in."

"Thanks," I mumble, looking around. The boxes of my things are still littering the foyer—we were going to unpack when we returned from our honeymoon. His apartment is sleek and modern, massive by city standards.

"Let me get you some coffee," he says hurriedly, rushing to the kitchen.

I nod and wander to the wall of windows overlooking Central Park. The sun is up fully now, casting an orange glow on the smog that always covers the city in the morning. Below, I can see cabs and town cars and busses maneuvering through traffic, tiny people scurrying every direction. Something twists in my chest.

"Verity," Henry says, pulling me from my thoughts. He gestures for me to join him on his white, leather sofa.

"Thank you." I accept the coffee from him and settle down. The sofa squeaks as I sit, something that never bothered me before.

Henry is quiet, watching me sip my coffee. When he finally speaks, his voice is soft, "I was starting to think you were dead."

I press my lips into a nervous line. "I'm sorry."

"What happened? Why are you dressed like that?" Henry asks, the questions pouring from his mouth.

"I was taken on our wedding day, abducted," I sigh heavily. I don't even know where to begin. It's all so unbelievable.

"That's what I thought." Henry stares down at his hands. "When we went looking for you all we found was a shoe and your bouquet."

"I must have dropped them," I say.

Henry looks up, his blue eyes fierce. "Who did this? How did you get away?"

"He let me go. He didn't do anything bad to me," I say hurriedly.

"We have to go to the police so they can catch this guy." Henry slips off the sofa and gets on his knees in front of me. He takes my hands in his. "I'm glad you're alright. I was so scared."

"How are my parents?" I ask, blinking back tears.

"They're okay, they'll be so relieved to know you're home." Henry kisses one of my knuckles. "I can call them up right now, we'll all fly to Vegas and we can get married there. We don't need the fairytale wedding."

"What?" I feel as if the wind has been knocked out of me.

Henry squeezes my hands tightly, too tightly. "When you went missing, I realized that I didn't care about all that stuff. I just cared about you. You've been all over the news, I've had people all around the country looking for you. Our wedding will bring us both closure, and it's a great way to end our story."

"Story?" I echo, brows furrowing.

"The bride who was kidnapped on her wedding day is a hot topic," Henry says, smiling kindly.

I slip my hands out of his and smooth my hair back. "Henry, I have to tell you something."

His face falls. "Oh, god. Did he rape you? Are you pregnant?"

"What?" I shake my head vigorously. "No, of course not. He wouldn't do that."

"He wouldn't do that?" Henry rises and stares out the window. "You seem to know a lot about what this man would and wouldn't do."

"I've been with him for weeks now," I say. My skirts rustle as I stand and move to Henry's side.

"Been with him?" He asks, his voice cold.

My spine stiffens, a shiver trailing down it. I know that tone. "Not like that, obviously."

"Did you fall in love with him?" He snaps.

"No, Henry, that's not it," I stammer.

He laughs, a chilling sound. "Tell me, did he dress you up like this? Buy you jewels? Did you find someone richer than me to manipulate?"

"Henry," I breathe, hurt straining my voice. "That's not how it was between us. My feelings were real."

The scowl slips away from his face, replaced by a loving expression. He reaches for me, running a hand over my cheek. "I'm sorry. I shouldn't be jealous of the man who took you against your will."

"No, you shouldn't," I say.

Henry wanders away, rambling about Vegas and which news outlets he'll invite. I don't know how to tell him. And what's worse, I'm afraid to tell him. Afraid because he can be volatile. But I have to tell him. I take a deep breath and move into the kitchen, closer to the front door.

"Henry," I say, loudly enough to interrupt him. "I still have to tell you something."

"Go ahead, darling." He smiles, his fingers hovering over his phone.

I inhale sharply. "Henry I can't marry you." The words tumble out of my mouth abandon.

He's silent for a moment before his eyes narrow. "What?"

"I can't marry you," I repeat, clenching my hands together.

"You're distraught from the terror of your experience," he says. "You don't know what you're saying."

"Yes, I do," I say insistently. "Henry, I can't marry you. Things have changed for me since I've been gone. I feel differently about you and about my life. I have to do what's best for me."

He laughs humorlessly. "You're not going anywhere."

I narrow my eyes at him. "What?"

"The kidnapped bride leaving the heartbroken groom is not the way this story ends," he hisses. "You will marry me."

"Drag me up to that altar and I'll say no," I snap.

Henry glowers at me. He stalks through the kitchen towards me, but I hold my ground. "I have done everything for you," he growls. "You would be nothing without me. You would be living in that hole in the wall in Brooklyn with no savings. Your parents will be in debt for the rest of their lives without me."

"That's something I'll have to live with." I back away from him, eyes narrowed.

Suddenly, his fist is raised above me, his face is red with anger. Fear courses through me, I've never been hit by a man before. I close my eyes and imagine that Altair bursts through the door. I imagine that he snatches Henry's wrist and breaks it with a simple squeeze. I imagine that he whisks me out of this apartment and back to the portal, wherever it is now.

But when I open my eyes, Altair isn't there. And Henry is still hovering over me. The rage in his eyes fades slowly as I stare at him. He lowers his arm, though his fist is still clenched at his side. "Get out," he croaks. "I don't want to see you again. I'll leave your shit on the sidewalk for you to pick up."

"Donate it," I say, my hand already on the doorknob. "Where I'm going, I don't need it."

CHAPTER 15

ALTAIR

Blood spurts from the Bloodbane witch's throat, coating my claws in hot, sticky liquid. I soar upwards into the bright blue sky before wheeling around for another attack. My men are on the ground, fighting against the Bloodbane witches that have crossed our borders yet again. The clang of their swords against the witches' daggers is loud. Dressed in light, golden armor, my soldiers stand bright against the maroon of the witches' cloaks.

The witches have grown more brazen since Maaz made her appearance at the ball. This is the largest group that has ever been spotted so close to Desmarais. A coven of fifty witches equipped with their poison arrows and daggers. I grit my teeth, picturing Maaz in my mind. She's behind this little invasion. It's a message to me that she will have what she wants; my kingdom.

I dart towards the ground, wings pinned to my back. The witches shout, and a volley of arrows flies towards me. I clip my wings out enough to direct my drop and avoid the poisonous tips, darting between them. Just a few meters off the ground, I spread my wings to stop my fall and glide over the Bloodbanes. I snatch one of them in my jaws and crush her spine. She squeals before falling abruptly silent.

I toss her aside and her body falls back to the ground with a sickening thud. I bank right, towards a Bloodbane in the back of the fight, staying out of the fray. She's working on a spell; I can smell it in the air—something burning. I streak towards her, claws outstretched. The witch pivots, her hood falling down to her shoulders. She's young, barely out of adolescence. That doesn't stop my claws from shredding through her.

My heart clenches in my chest as her corpse falls to the ground. She didn't look much younger than Verity. Of course, the witch was far older in truth, but in the terms of immortality, she was young. Too young for death. The battle is winding down, the last of the Bloodbane witches turning on their heels and running back towards the mountain border.

I land and shake out my blood-spattered wings. Pine needles and dirt stick to my paws, glued to the blood. Corpses dot the clearing in the dense forest where our battle took place. My soldiers pick through them, dragging the Fae who fell in battle away from the Bloodbane bodies. We'll bring the soldiers back to Desmarais for a proper funeral. And for the Bloodbanes we build a funeral pyre.

We watch their corpses slowly burn to ash as the flames lick at the blue sky. This was only a single battle, there will be more before the curse runs its course. And after that, there will be no one left to protect Desmarais and my kingdom, Alnembra, from Maaz. I will be gone, and so will many of my people. Almost two thousand years of existence, gone in the blink of an eye. Unless Verity returns.

I shake my head, turning away from the pyre. Verity won't be returning. One of Navi's lieutenants' approaches, a Fae man named Rynt. "Your Grace, we're ready to return with the fallen," he says, his brown eyes somber.

I peer past him towards the three corpses in golden armor. "Very well."

Rynt snaps a salute before returning to the soldiers. Wordlessly, they march out of the clearing in perfect form, the bodies of their comrades on stretchers between them. I watch them disappear through the foliage before launching myself into the sky. A sense of gloom has fallen over the palace and Desmarais since Verity's departure, I'm not immune either.

The rage has faded, but the sorrow remains. I had high hopes that Verity could truly break the curse. We were making progress; she was opening up to me and learning to trust me. Her sudden rejection left me nursing my ego and worse, trying to find another way to break the curse. I've had a thousand years to find a solution, and Verity was the only one. My scholars worked tirelessly to find her, but she slipped from my fingers so quickly. No. I let her slip from my fingers.

The palace comes into view ahead of me, but it looks dimmer than before. Somehow, knowing Verity isn't there makes it seem empty. I drop into the courtyard, a few feet from Navi. She looks me over emotionless. "How many?" She asks, falling into stride beside me.

"Fifty," I say, stifling a yawn. "They're growing bolder."

"I'll double the patrol units on the border and in the guard towers," Navi says, and I'm sure she already gave the order before I even arrived. "You have a guest in the gardens."

"A guest?" I shake out my feathers. "Is it one of my advisers here to berate me for losing the precious Key?"

Navi strides away, towards the barracks. "The gardens."

I roll my eyes at the commanding tone of her voice but launch myself into the air. I skim over the trees that surround the courtyard towards the gardens in the back of the castle. There are several gardens on the grounds; a rose garden, a water garden, and a wild garden. I scan the gardens as I soar over them, searching for any sign of my advisers or the mysterious guest.

As I skim across the hedged walls of the wild garden, my heart skips a beat. Verity's light brown hair glimmers in the sun as she stoops over a book. She glances up at the sound of my wings, and blocks the sun from her eyes, searching for me. Relief floods through me at the sight of her as I land nearby. She twists, dressed in the oversized trousers and shirt that she usually wears. She's lovely.

I head towards her, grateful that she can't read the expressions on my face when I'm in this form. I'm afraid that would give away how much joy I feel at the sight of her. She closes her book as I approach, placing it on top of a nearby stack.

"You came back," I say softly.

She smiles tentatively. "Don't sound so surprised. I told you I would come back before I left."

"I didn't believe you." I sit beside her, cocking my head. "What about your fiancé?"

"I don't have one anymore," she says casually. Her eyes lock onto mine, as blue as the sky above us.

"Why not?" I ask. I break her gaze and pretend to take in the wild garden.

The wild garden is an apt name for this place. My mother had it planted when she was Queen. She filled it with every flower or blooming tree that ever took her fancy and the gardeners let them grow with wild abandon. Verity found one of the few grassy lawns in the garden, right beside a small koi pond. In such beautiful surroundings, Verity fits in perfectly.

"I didn't love him. I never did," she says, sighing.

I look curiously at her. "Then why were you marrying him?"

"My parents were in debt up to their eye balls and he promised me that he would pay it all for them if I married him," Verity explains, picking at the blades of grass. "It sounds terrible, but I was just trying to help my parents."

"I understand," I say. I stretch out on the grass beside her.

"Why did you really come back? You were in your world, in your home. You could have stayed."

Verity edges closer to me, her eyes drifting over my body. "I'm not sure why I came back. But I do want to help you. I want to break your curse; protect you from Maaz."

My heart swells in my chest at her words, happiness coursing through me. This is a step. I nod my head, hiding the happiness I feel. "There may be hope yet."

"I still don't know what to do," she says quickly. "But I'm willing to keep trying."

"My people and I are at your disposal," I murmur.

We fall silent and Verity shifts uncomfortably on her knees before finally falling back into a sitting position. She reaches for one of her books. "Should we continue the book?" She asks, waving it at me.

I study the cover and groan. "The romance?"

"The romance," she confirms. "We have to finish it before we start the next one."

"And how many books are there?" I ask, dreading her answer.

She grins wickedly. "Five."

"Oh, gods," I groan. "Fine."

I lay down beside her as she falls onto her back, the book lifted above her face. My head is beside hers, and my breath ruffles her hair with each exhale. She reads, her melodic voice ringing through the garden. I imagine that every tree and every flower leans closer to hear. The story itself is a poorly written rendering of a classic myth in Alnembra; the tale of the nymph that fell in love with Sadal Melik, the Dark God.

But I don't read with Verity for the stories. I listen to her read because I love the sound of her voice. I love the way she struggles to pronounce our words and names but never blushes with embarrassment. I love the way her face shows every reaction to the story, whether she knows it or not. I love that she's chosen to spend time with me.

I close my eyes, letting the soft lilt of her voice lull me to sleep. My body aches from the battle and I'm exhausted from the rage and sorrow I felt when she left. All I want to do is sleep. I hear her shift beside me, rolling, and I open a sleepy eye. Her gaze breaks away from the page for an instant to look at me, but she never stops her narration. When she looks away, I let my eye slip closed again, assured that she's still beside me.

The words she reads mean nothing to me as I doze, only the sound of her voice. The grass is soft beneath me, the perfect cushion for me to rest on. The garden is filled with the singing of birds and the lapping of the pond beside me. I purr softly as her cool fingers stroke my head rhythmically. The last thing I remember before I fall asleep entirely is her voice.

CHAPTER 16

Altair blinks sleepily at me as he wakes. I arch a brow at him, the book still open in my hands. He fell asleep almost an hour ago, snoring softly. Altair stretches like a cat, his claws extending from his paws. Specks of dried blood coat his claws and I drop my gaze back to my books.

"Leaving?" He yawns, watching me gather the books.

I stand, grunting as I pick up the stack of thick books. "Going to help me?"

He grins. "As you can see, I'm powerless to save you from those heavy texts."

"Of course you are." I roll my eyes. "I'll see you at dinner."

"I won't be at dinner tonight," Altair says. I turn, surprise flickering in my eyes. He lounges back and dangles one of his massive paws in the pond. "Come to my room after the sun sets."

"Why?" I ask warily.

Altair turns his hazel eyes to me. "Because I want to see you again."

My heart does backflips in my chest at his words, warmth rushing to my cheeks. "I'll think about it."

I turn away and hurry from the garden back to the library. We both know what my answer will be. I can feel Altair's eyes on me as I disappear through the hedge gate. A moment later, his shadow streaks over the ground ahead of me as he soars away past the castle turrets. Since I've been here, Altair hasn't missed dinner once. I bite my lip, wondering what he might be doing. He might simply be skipping dinner with me to spite me for leaving. I wouldn't put it past him, I smile to myself.

Three guards are posted in the library, and one stations himself beside the door when I enter. Altair seems to have been shaken by Maaz's visit. I drop my books onto a nearby table. The librarian hasn't taught me the Fae shelving system yet, but she promised me she would. It will be a good way to spend my time, since I'm sequestered to the palace.

I sigh and search through the bookshelves for any texts I haven't read yet pertaining to magic and curses. I wish I had been clever enough to question the Bloodbane witches about the curse more. I should have. Anxiety twists my stomach as I think about Altair and the curse. He hasn't pressured me with his timeline, but I know that time is running short. And I haven't made any progress.

I release a deep breath, glancing out the window as the sun is setting. Whatever Altair is occupied with, it will keep him for a few more hours. I settle into an armchair in the library with books on the Bloodbane history and lose myself in them. At least I try. My thoughts wander to Altair as I my eyes roam the pages.

I know I did the right thing leaving Henry. My brief visit with him proved that to me. I'm not a story for him to boost his celebrity or a trophy for him to wear on his arm. Henry never could understand that, and now I see it clearly. Altair didn't even put me on display during the ball; my time in the spotlight was brief, and it seemed meaningless to him.

I purse my lips. It's hard to come to terms with the fact that

Altair is using me just as Henry was using me. And like I was using Henry. Is that what relationships are? Two people using each other? I trail my finger across the words of the page, eyes staring blankly. My only relief is that I'm not using Altair. Not yet anyway.

The clock strikes, drawing me from my reverie. My eyes snap towards the window, the darkness is all encompassing. Quickly, I set my books aside and uncurl from the chair. I consider going back to my room and changing into something more elegant for Altair but change my mind as I climb the steps. He probably doesn't care what I wear. And I don't care what he thinks of what I wear, I lie to myself.

His door is cracked open, light spilling through it into the hall. Navi doesn't stand guard outside as she usually does, and I wonder why. I slip through the cracked door and close it softly behind me. Altair's back is to me as he bends over a heavy wooden table in the center of the room. I admire him, his muscles shifting beneath the long-sleeved tunic he wears.

"Did you get anything to eat?" He asks, twisting to look at me.

I bite my lip under his hazel gaze. "No."

He gestures for me to come closer. "Good, I had some food brought up for us."

"I thought you said no dinner?" I cock a brow, moving to his side.

The air between us is warm. My elbow grazes his arm and his eyes slip across my face with an expression I can't read. "You truly are never satisfied, are you?" He asks, though a smile plays across his lips.

"I could be," I say defensively, perusing the food spread across the table. I pluck a sweet bun from one of the plates. "What are you doing?"

He leans to the side so I can see the map laid out in front of him. "Looking at my kingdom. My home."

His voice carries a melancholy edge to it. "Saying goodbye to it already?" I ask, keeping my voice soft.

"Just in case," he whispers. He traces a river with an elegant finger.

"Will you die if I don't break the curse?" We've never discussed the curse much. I never thought it would end in anything sinister, but after seeing Maaz—I wonder if I was wrong.

He nods. "I will. And so will my people."

"Everyone?" My voice cracks.

Altair's hazel eyes bore into me. "I spent hundreds of years looking for you, Verity."

"Altair." I drop his gaze, a feeling of anguish washing over me.

I wander to the balcony, brows furrowed. I stare out at Desmarais beneath us, the city that stretches from the cliff faces below to the sea in the distance. The city lights glimmer in the darkness, some soft music reaches my ears from below. It isn't nearly as vibrant as it was when I first saw it. There's a gloom that hangs over it now.

"All those people," I murmur. "Maaz would kill them all. Why?"

Altair makes a choking sound, and I whirl to face him. He lifts his hands, gesturing for me to stay back. "My hands are tied," he croaks out.

"I won't ask any more questions," I say hurriedly, face crumpled with worry.

He's silent for a moment, lips twisting in sorrow and frustration. He comes back to himself and stands tall, straightening his tunic. "I'm sorry. I didn't ask you to come tonight to pass my burden to you. Or sadden you."

"Why did you ask me to come tonight?" I move to the table and trail a finger over the gleaming wood.

"I'm curious about you," he says simply.

"Curious?" I stop by his side, staring up at him.

His eyes gleam as he meets my gaze and his nostrils flare. "Why did you come back?"

"We can't talk about the curse, remember?" I smirk. "Ask me something else."

"Ah, this game," he says softly.

"This game," I echo, curling into an arm chair by the fireplace.

He joins me, slinging an ankle over his knee. He looks thoughtfully at me, a finger tapping his arm rest. "What did you do before I brought you here?"

A laugh bursts from my lips. "I was a librarian at an inner-city high school. I helped students do research and I kept the library in order."

"That explains your love for reading," he muses.

"My turn." I shift, tucking my legs beneath me and leaning towards him. "Tell me about your parents."

"That's not a question." Altair smirks.

"Tell me anyway," I say, crumpling my brows. "Please."

Altair shudders dramatically. "Your pleading is rather unsightly."

I glower at him. "Unsightly?"

"I'm teasing," he reassures me. "Though it doesn't suit you. It doesn't suit you at all."

I purse my lips, wondering what he really means. "Are you going to tell me or not?"

"So demanding," he huffs. He leans forward, the light of the fire illuminating his handsome features. "There isn't much to tell. My mother was arranged to marry my father when they were young, around six hundred years old. They ruled together for almost three thousand years before they died on their way to a neighboring kingdom. The ship was caught in a storm and they drowned. Their bodies were never found. I took the throne then, but I was young and rash. That's when Maaz came."

"I'm so sorry," I whisper, searching his eyes. I find little sorrow in them.

He sniffs, leaning back. "It was a long time ago."

"Still." I cock my head. "I can imagine that losing a parent is hard. Let alone two."

Altair's lip curls and I feel a flash of fear. "I've never felt comfortable with pity."

My brows twitch together, and I press my lips into a thin, angry line. "When someone offers their condolences, it isn't pity, Altair. It's sympathy. And you should get used to pity. Because if the curse takes you, there will be no one left to pity you but me."

As soon as the words leave my lips, I feel a wave of guilt and shame. Altair's sneer fades away as the silence draws out between us. I close my eyes, cursing myself for speaking harshly. I don't like being snapped at for trying to be kind, but that doesn't mean I can be cruel. Especially not to Altair. Because whether I like it or not, I feel an irresistible urge to be near him. To be close in more than just the physical sense.

I open my eyes, expecting to find Altair glaring at me. But he's crouched in front of me, staring knowingly at me. "Are you finished?" He asks, arching a brow.

I nod hesitantly and sigh. "Alta-," I say.

But he cuts me off, pressing his lips against mine fiercely. My entire being explodes with brilliant light and flame as he cups my face in his hands. I lean into him and my fingers find a purchase on his shoulders. I dig my fingers into his muscles, clutching at him. His lips are soft and warm and fierce. Our lips move as one and I imagine that our hearts beat to the same rhythm.

A small gasp escapes me as I feel his tongue dart across my bottom lip. But he doesn't take the kiss any further than that. He kisses me as if he just needed to know that I'm real. That I'm here with him. So, I curl my fingers around his cheeks, feeling the short bristles of his facial hair. Desire floods through me. I want more than this. My body desperately needs more from him, and I know I want it just as much. Whatever it is that I feel for Altair, it's only heightened by the tender way he kisses me.

He pulls away, panting, but doesn't release my face. Altair stares deeply into my eyes, his lips slightly parted. I know my cheeks are flushed, and that I'm breathing just as heavily. For what feels like hours, we simply stare at one another and I imagine he can see right into my soul. Right into my deepest thoughts and desires. And they all revolve around him.

Finally, his hands slip away from my face and he moves back. "I'm sorry," he says, not sounding very apologetic at all. "But I had to punish you for your insolent tone."

I gape at him. But despite the outrage on my face, I feel a tendril of excitement at his words. "You're unbelievable."

He bites his lip and then grins at me. "I believe it's my turn in the game."

"Fine," I sigh, falling back into the chair. I shake my head and roll my eyes as he settles into his own arm chair.

"If you weren't a librarian, what would you do?" He asks.

"Indiana Jones," I blurt.

"Indiana Jones?" His brows furrow in confusion. "What is this?"

I pluck at a stray thread on my trousers. "Not what; who."

Altair is quiet and curious as I launch into my explanation of the famous adventuring archaeologist. He insists that I tell him the stories and our game of questions quickly devolves into an argument about Jones.

"Must the woman always die?" Altair asks, anger tinging his voice.

I laugh. "Well not always, but it's a simple way to make sure he can have a love interest later."

Altair grumbles under his breath but doesn't stop me as I plunge back into the forays of Dr. Jones. He interrupts from time to time with questions, mostly surrounding the artifacts in the stories. I do my best to explain and Altair catches on quickly.

The more I speak, the more his eyes soften, and we find ourselves leaning imperceptibly towards each other. My gaze drops to his lips, quirked into a smile. I want to save Altair, but I don't know how. And if I can't, I don't want to spend the rest of my life pining after a man I couldn't save. So, I keep my distance, and focus my attention on the stories.

If I save him, maybe I could open up to him more. Maybe this could be something. But then again, I'll die in another seventy years at most. And Altair will live on for thousands. I falter, my sentence fading into silence.

"What is it?" Altair asks.

I drag my eyes away from the flames to meet his worried gaze. "I should go. It's getting late."

"It's barely ten," he says, eyes narrowing.

"Just let me go, Altair," I snap, rising.

He presses his lips together. Silently, he waves towards the door. I rush past him, but his hand snakes out and snatches my writs. I yelp as he pulls me backward into his lap. With my legs draped over the arm rest, I strain my neck to keep upright. His face hovers over mine, an intelligent gleam in his eyes.

"What are you doing?" I ask, voice strained.

"More punishment for presuming to tell the King what to do," he purrs.

A thrill courses through me, heating blooming in my body. I stare at him with wide eyes, expecting him to kiss me. But he doesn't. Altair drags a finger from my temple down my cheek. I shiver as he trails it down my neck and along my ribs. When my breath hitches in my throat as his finger runs along my thigh, he grins wickedly.

Suddenly, he has me upright, hair disheveled and mouth gaping. He eyes me from the chair, propping his chin in his hand. "Goodnight, Verity," he murmurs.

I blink at him and force my body to move. Walking stiffly, I manage to make it out of his room before turning a bright shade of pink. He knows exactly what he does to me. I bite my lip, picturing the delicious smirk he wore as he teased me. My heart is beating wildly, emotions running rampant. Everything I do, every moment I spend with him, only brings us closer. It's a dangerous place to be; close to Altair. But I don't want it any other way, I realize as my heart pounds. How much longer can I convince myself that I don't want him?

CHAPTER 17

Altair

I'm beginning to wonder if it will ever get boring teasing Verity. I doubt it. Somehow, she always manages to surprise me with her reactions. The moment I expect her to lash out at me, she'll blush prettily instead. I stretch my wings behind me, letting the wind ruffle through the silky feathers. Since the ball, all I've been able to think about is Verity.

It was on this tower that I first learned of Verity's existence from Navi. This is the place I would come to when I felt the most discouraged about the curse. It was here that I would look out over Desmarais and curse myself for failing them. But Verity has brought me hope. And now the tower has become just another place, rather than the pillar of all my fears.

I bask in the light of the rising sun. It's high summer now, and soon all of Alnembra will celebrate the Summer's Eve. I didn't think any of us would be alive to celebrate, but perhaps we will. I lay my wings back on the stony floor, letting them splay out beside me. How much longer will I have these wings? How much longer will I be tethered to this beast that Maaz drew out from within me? I'm beginning to think that I'll miss it.

But Verity isn't mine yet. But I know I can't pressure her. She must choose to bind herself to me of her own free will. I can only hope that she realizes the key to breaking the curse has nothing to do with potions and spells and everything to do with the covenant of our blood.

I stare out over Desmarais, the beautiful city of glass. The pink light of the rising sun reflects vibrantly off of the rooftops and the sea in the distance. It's alight with a warm glow, the kind of view that sets your heart on fire. I don't want to leave Desmarais. I don't want my legacy to be that I let all of Alnembra suffer because of the rash words of a young Fae.

I was up all night thinking of Verity. I came to this tower to get a glimpse of my land and my kingdom, hoping it would clear my head. But now all I can think is that I want to share this view with Verity. I want to share my city with her. But until she's safe from Maaz, I can't. I stretch out my claws as my thoughts tray to Maaz.

As I think of Maaz, the view of my city just becomes another scene in the background. I remember the first time I saw her. She swept past me on her deadwood broom, straight to the doors of the palace and demanded an audience with my father. I don't know what passed between them, but Maaz left in a fury and my mother kept me inside for almost a week. It drove me mad. But then I put Maaz from my thoughts and I never thought of her again until nine hundred and ninety-nine years ago when she made another appearance.

I clench my jaw irately as I picture the moment she doomed me and my people. A simple request, she had said. Grant it to me, King. Marry me. Marry me and join our bloodlines. We'll have the most powerful children the world has ever known. And when I refused her, she cursed me. With fury in her eyes she cursed me to this existence.

I can feel the rage swelling in my chest, coursing through my veins as I remember the torture Maaz has inflicted on me. My claws dig into the stone, scratching white marks across the dark floor. I consider leaping off of the parapet and flying to Maaz's stronghold in the mountains. But if I do that, the curse takes immediate effect and I lose everything I've worked to save these last thousand years.

Suddenly, I hear Verity's musical laughter echo towards me. I blink, surprised. The anger fades away when I hear her laugh again. I peer over the edge of the tower and see her in the gardens. Like a miniature version of herself, she seems so small from up here. I watch as she walks with one of the soldiers I assigned to guard her. He speaks, though I can't make out the words. Verity places a hand on his elbow as she giggles in response.

Instantly, my blood is on fire in my veins. My vision tunnels to her hand, touching him, and all I hear is her laughter echoing round and round in my head. Without thinking, I launch myself from the tower and swoop towards them. The soldier hears me coming before Verity, and he steps away to a discrete distance. I glide over them, claws out, and hear Verity yelp as she ducks.

When I land, I turn a cold gaze towards the soldier. "Take a walk," I snarl, eyes flashing.

He dips into a bow before jogging away, his armor clanking. Verity approaches, her lips pursed. "What was that about?" She asks, crossing her arms over her chest.

I stare at her hands, partially hidden in the folds of her arm. The hands that touched another man. "I could ask you the same thing," I say quietly, pacing around her.

"What are you talking about?" She sighs exasperatedly. "I was talking a walk in the gardens, but a guard came with me. I was fine."

"You certainly looked more than fine from where I was standing." I circle her, my hazel eyes raking over her body.

She turns in a slow circle, always facing me as I pace. Her

cheeks color, which only sends more thoughts of envy through my mind. "That was nothing. Is that what this is about?"

"It didn't look like nothing," I growl, closing in on her. "I saw you touch him. Heard you laughing."

"He's nice, I was talking to him," Verity snaps. She backs up against a tree, her eyes wide as I approach.

"Just talking?" I ask softly. I nudge her hand with my nose. I can smell him on her. "Don't let anyone touch you except for me."

I hear her heart racing as my eyes drift over her body. "Why?" She whispers.

I growl quietly. I want to roar that she's mine, but I know Verity well enough to know that she wouldn't take kindly to such possession. But the jealousy is still coursing through me, particularly as his scent permeates the air between us. It was only a single touch, but it was enough.

Fae men are territorial when they fall in love. It can't be avoided and despite our wisdom, we've never managed to overcome it. I meet her gaze and stare resolutely at her. "I don't know if I can trust even my own men," I say finally.

She raises a brow suspiciously. "Alright."

"Good," I sigh, taking a step back. The tension has eased somewhat, but I know I won't ever be able to get this out of my mind.

"Can I go now?" She asks, pushing away from the tree and stepping around me.

"Go," I manage to say, even though every cell in my body is straining against the words. Stay. Stay. Stay.

But she leaves. Across the lawn, she glances at me over her shoulder. I imagine I see a flicker of a smile on her lips before she disappears into the castle. I run my tongue over my teeth and dig my claws into the dirt before I throw myself into the sky. It takes only a moment to find the man who touched her as I follow his scent around the castle grounds.

I find him in the courtyard of the barracks, beside Navi. I land heavily beside him, not bothering to slow to avoid colliding with anyone. He doesn't appear surprised to see me. I stare at him, marking that my paw is the same size as his face. How easily I could crush him, even with all that armor.

Navi glances between the two of us but doesn't interrupt. The soldier salutes me, snapping his spear to his side. "Your Grace," he barks.

"Don't ever touch her again," I growl. "If you touch her, I will tear the offending limb from your body without a second thought."

"Yes, Your Grace," the soldier says, his eyes boring holes into the wall.

I snap my teeth at him, enjoying the way his face pales. "Leave." The soldier obeys without another word and I turn to Navi. "I want him reassigned. Latrine duty or something equally unpleasant."

She stares at me, amusement twinkling in her green eyes. "I'll assign him to the boardwalk."

The boardwalk is a small quarter of Desmarais, the eastern docks. It's a cesspool of crime and the heart of Desmarais' underground. Navi has been trying to clear it out for much of her time as the Captain of the Guard, though with little success. Verity will never see that soldier if he's stationed there.

"Good," I concede.

Navi grows serious. "I've found no evidence of the spy, Altair."

"None?" I narrow my eyes. "Keep looking. If you must, have your most trusted men and women question everyone in the palace."

"I will, but I doubt we'll find anything." Her fingers wrap around the hilt of her blade tightly.

"Why not?" I ask.

"I haven't found anything of use yet, and I fear that the spy may have already left or is much more well hidden than I thought. We can't trust anyone. Not even Verity," she says slowly, carefully.

I scoff. "Verity? You truly think Verity might be the spy? That she may have organized her own kidnapping?"

"Perhaps." Navi shrugs. "We know little of her. It's only a theory, I will keep searching."

"Do. And Navi?" I flick my tail in irritation. "No unclaimed men or women in Verity's personal guard."

Navi cocks a brow and smirks. "Really, Altair? Don't you find that extreme?"

"No," I growl. "I truly don't."

Before Navi can reply, I leap onto the roof of the barracks and then into the air. I spread my wings and catch myself, soaring along the currents of the wind into the sky. Navi's words echo on my head as I fly across the palace grounds. I huff, I'm not being extreme. But it would be best if Verity doesn't know why I made rearrangements to her personal guard.

I find myself drifting towards the library, where I know she'll be. As I glide past, I see her, searching through a stack of books by the window. She glances up as my shadow falls over her. My heart lurches as our eyes meet, but soon she's out of my sight as I follow the curve of the castle walls.

These feelings are new to me. I've never felt this sort of possessiveness, I scoffed at the Fae who acted this way. But now, I understand all too well. I don't want to lose the warmth and light that I feel when I see Verity. I want that light only on me. Though I'm not sure that she feels the same way, and the thought is devastating to me. Sighing, I make another round around the castle—hoping for another glimpse of her.

I hope that soon she will crave me as much as I crave her. I hope that she will bind herself to me before it's too late.

CHAPTER 18

VERITY

I waddle away from the castle door and towards an unoccupied part of the lawn with the cauldron in my arms. It's heavy; iron, I'm guessing. My muscles are screaming as I carry it, wishing one of the Fae in my guard would be willing to help. But the Fae have sworn off magic, and they don't appear too keen on my practice.

With a grunt, I heave the cauldron onto the ground, careful not to crush my fingers. I catch my breath, hands on my hips, before turning back to the castle. I need to gather the ingredients for the potion I'm making. A potion of unbinding, I thought perhaps it could unbind Altair from the curse. I jog up the castle steps, catching a glimpse of Altair's wings disappearing over the gable.

I grin to myself as I tread down the halls. Altair has spent the day watching me, I wonder if he thinks he's being discrete. I saw him every time he passed the library window, his eyes locked onto me. I've never met a man as territorial as Altair, but there's something particularly animalistic about it. And something very appealing.

In the kitchen pantry, I run over the list of ingredients I need. "Powder of the titan arum, white baneberry, and root of ginseng," I mutter aloud as I study the shelves.

I pluck what I need and head back outside, ignoring the cold looks of the Fae. Magic of any kind, Bloodbane or not, is frowned upon here. I imagine it was different before the Bloodbane grew so powerful and cursed Altair. But I ignore their stares as I kneel beside the cauldron. Discouraged or not, I need to do all I can to save Altair.

I light a fire beneath the cauldron, grimacing as the flames burn the nearby grass. I pour water into the cauldron and wait patiently for it to boil. In an iron pot above a fire, it takes longer than it would at home. I sigh, staring into the cauldron. I can feel Altair's eyes on me. I glance up and see him perched on the gabled rooftop. I stick my tongue out at him and turn back to my cauldron; it's boiling.

Quickly I measure out a bit of titan arum powder, a red substance, and pour it into the boiling water. A puff of red smoke erupts from the pot, I wave it away, coughing. As the powder dissolves in the hot water, I grind the baneberry into mush. It can only be done immediately before I put them in the potion, or they lose their potency. Or so the text says.

The mush of the berries plops into the red potion and it turns a royal purple. Satisfied with my progress so far, I grin. Who would have thought that a librarian from New York City would be brewing potions outside a Fae king's castle? After letting it stew for a few minutes, I add the last ingredient.

The potion bubbles and a sickly-sweet smell floats upwards. My grin falls away as the overly sweet scent chokes my lungs. The sun is setting as I pull the cauldron from the flames and pour its contents into a glass bottle. I cap it and put it carefully in my pocket. The potion is still hot, warm enough that I can feel it against my leg. I pour the rest of the water onto the dwindling fire.

The grass beneath the charred wood is black, and likely dead. I grimace apologetically at the Fae nearby. Hoisting the warm cauldron into my arms, I struggle to carry it back into the castle. Suddenly, Altair appears by my side. He slips the cauldron from my arms without a word and falls into step beside me. I eye him, taking in his strong figure, dressed in simple black clothes. The vest he wears over his tunic is tailored to him well, showing the leanness of his strong frame.

I bite my bottom lip, hiding the tendril of excitement I feel when he's beside me. Altair's arm grazes against me heat blossoms through me. "What potion did you brew today?" He asks, his voice calm and strong.

"A potion of unbinding. I'm not sure how it will taste," I warn him as we enter the kitchens.

The cooks look up from dressing the dinner, but Altair gestures for them to continue. "I'll wash it down with a large glass of wine," he says, flashing me a grin.

I watch as he rinses the cauldron in the stone sink and sets it aside. He's more thoughtful than I realized. "And does the King often do dishes?" I ask, arching a brow.

"That depends, how appealing do you find it?" He counters.

"Very," I purr. Before he can answer, I take the stairs two at a time, leaving him at the landing. I call over my shoulder, "I'll meet you for dinner."

"I'll be waiting," he says, chuckling.

I can feel his eyes watching me as I round the corner and disappear from view. Tingles slip down my spine and I suppress a shiver. Whenever I feel his eyes on me it's as if I'm back in that armchair, breathless and filled with cravings.

In my room, I strip quickly; carefully setting the potion aside. I already picked out a gown for dinner, a sea blue dress with long, sheer sleeves. I slip into it, easily buttoning myself in as the back is bare. I study myself in the mirror and brush my hair back self-consciously. This will have to do.

Grabbing the potion, I go to our private dining hall to join him. My stomach is in knots that I can't explain as I push open the door. Altair is already there, standing beside the fireplace. He turns as the door creaks, and his lips split into a smile. A real, genuine, and tender smile. My heart pounds faster.

"Shall we start dinner off with a bang?" He asks, pulling my chair out for me.

"What?" I gape, cheeks coloring.

His brows furrow. "The potion. Shall I have it now?"

"Oh." I close my eyes and silently berate myself for having my mind in the gutter. But Altair does that to me sometimes. "Here, try it."

He plucks the glass bottle from my hands and moves around the table. This time, he's moved the flowers from between us. Now I have nothing to hide behind. I pour myself a glass of wine as he uncorks the bottle. He stares into the potion and then quirks a brow. "Wish me luck."

As Altair downs the potion, his brows furrow with disgust. But he drinks it all, his throat bobbing with each gulp. I bite my lip as he lowers the bottle from his lips and pinches his face. A part of me didn't think he would actually drink the potion I brewed. I thought he would scoff at me like the other Fae. Altair slams the bottle onto the table, grimacing.

"Wine," he croaks.

I pass him my glass hastily and he chugs it, eyes clenched tightly closed. "Are you okay?" I ask, worry and fear forcing my voice to a higher pitch.

He coughs, returning my glass. "Fine," he finally manages to say. He stares at the glass bottle and shudders. "What was that?"

I list off the ingredients. "If it works, your eyes will change color."

"Care to check?" He asks, pushing the glass bottle aside as if it's poison.

"You don't sound too convinced," I say, moving around the table until I'm directly in front of him.

"Shall I stand? Or sit?" He asks.

"Sit." I bend down and peer into his eyes, our faces only inches apart.

His breath wafts over my face, smelling faintly of wine and berries. "You're working hard, Verity. But perhaps the solution is simpler than you think," he murmurs.

"Simpler?" I echo softly. His eyes are hazel, just as they were before. But still, I don't want to move away from him. If anything, I want to close the distance between us and kiss him fiercely. But I hold back, hovering over his lips.

"I can't tell you anything more than that," he says softly. "But perhaps the witches who kidnapped you had more to say, if you can remember."

"I'll try," I breathe, searching his dilated eyes.

"Verity," he murmurs, a hoarse edge to his voice. "Do you intend to hover over me all night? I can think of other ways we could spend our time if you enjoy being on top."

I blush and lurch away from him, heart pounding. "I'm sure you could," I quip.

His tongue runs over his lips and he takes a deep, shuddering breath as I return to my seat. "You really shouldn't tempt me, Verity."

"Tempt you?" I arch a brow as our food is brought to us.

His hazel eyes rake over me. "Fae men can be quite feral."

My eyes widen, a thrill coursing through me. "Duly noted," I murmur.

We lapse into silence, only the sound of cutlery against the porcelain plates and the crackling of the fire fill the air. I steal glances of Altair from time to time, when I dare. But he's always looking back at me. Looking at me with intensity that sends my heart racing wildly and my mind spiraling. I shake my head. I hated Altair, hated him from the moment I met him. Things changed quickly for me.

"So," I say, breaking the silence. "What did you today besides spy on me?"

His eyes flash, a smile playing across his lips. "Unfortunately, that took up almost all of my time."

"I would have thought a King had more to do than that," I say.

"A King of a dying kingdom?" He quirks a brow, but I don't miss the sorrow in his eyes. "Not quite."

"Do you miss it?" I ask, lowering my voice. "Ruling and planning for the future like you did before the curse?"

Altair sighs through his nose and downs his glass of wing. "I miss it every day."

"Tell me what it was like." I rest my chin in my hand, suddenly curious. There's so much I don't know about Altair, and what this place was like before Maaz tried to destroy it.

"It was tiring," Altar says, leaning back in his chair as his face takes on a faraway look. "I spent long hours of the day meeting with my people, trying to resolve their everyday problems. And after that I met with my councilors, the lords of the kingdom. We planned new expansions to the economy, new guard posts on the border, everything and anything."

"And there were women fawning over you, of course," I say, eyes glittering.

"Oh, so many women," he teases. He grows serious, locking eyes with me. "I haven't been with anyone in hundreds of years."

I raise my brows. "Some people can't go a month."

"Time is different for the Fae." He shrugs. Altair rises and moves to a bench beside the window. He pats the seat beside him, arching a brow expectantly. Sighing, I push away from the table and join him. "Look at it," he murmurs.

I follow his gaze out the window, towards the lights of Desmarais. "It's beautiful," I say, tilting my head. The city is awash in sapphire darkness, lit like a jewelry box. It sparkles in the dark, vibrant with life.

"Imagine what it looked like a thousand years ago, at the peak of my rule." He taps the glass. "It was a hundred times brighter than that. You could hear the music and laughter from here."

"You miss it," I say, a statement rather than a question.

"I do." He nods. "I would do anything to get it back."

I smile softly. "Like kidnap a woman."

He eyes me, cocking his head. "I would steal you away a million times if it saved my people."

"I know you would," I murmur, heart racing. I might even let him.

"Verity," he says softly. I meet his gaze and my blood runs faster at the fire in his eyes. "Are you happy here?"

I purse my lips thoughtfully. "I am," I finally say, nodding.

"And do I make you happy?" His voice is hoarse, eyebrows crumpled. He looks vulnerable.

My lips part in surprise at his question, and at the somberness of his tone. I inhale sharply. "I suppose," I say, voice faltering.

He breaks out into a relieved smile and leans his head against the cold windowpane. "Thank you, Verity."

"For what?" I furrow my brows. But Altair doesn't answer, he simple stares out at his city. "Tell me more about it. Life before the curse, I mean."

Altair's eyes snap towards me and his smile broadens. "It may take all night."

"I think we can risk a sleepless night." I settle back, my knees touching his.

Altair speaks then, his voice low and melodic. He tells me of parties filled with light and sound, colors that I've never even dreamed of. He tells me about the ships that used to sail in and out of his harbor at all hours, their massive sails blocking the moon. He tells me about the emissaries from exotic Fae kingdoms that traveled to Desmarais to see the breathtaking city and forge alliances with its strong King.

And as he speaks, my eyes drift closed. I feel his fingers gently stroking my arms, trailing fire and tingling pleasure along my skin. He's still murmuring his history to me as sleep takes me and his arms ease me down into his lap. The last thing I remember is his hand, warm on my back.

CHAPTER 19

Altair

I heave a breath as the morning sun glistens over Desmarais' harbor. Splashes of pink and gold shimmer on the horizon. But the beauty of the sight does little to curb my sorrow. The city is quiet, the street shops and boutiques closed. No ships linger at the docks. It might as well be a town haunted by spirits and wraiths.

I tap my claws against the stone of the tower as I hear Navi's footsteps on the stairs. She's quiet as she joins me, staring out at the once glorious city. "All the guards and servants have left," she murmurs.

I turn to her, taking her as if I've never seen her before. Dressed in a forest green cuirass and leathers, with her sword at her hip, she looks formidable and fierce. She's braided her auburn hair in a crown around her head for her last day on earth. She meets my gaze, her green eyes somber.

"Thank you, Navi," I say softly. "You may go home as well if you wish."

"This is my home," she says.

"I wish the end hadn't come so quickly," I sigh.

Navi stiffens her shoulders, eye twitching. "She had over a month to remedy the curse. It wasn't much time for her. Though I am disappointed, she doesn't seem as quick-witted as we hoped."

"She is," I snap. "Verity simply doesn't know. And has no one to turn to but useless books in that useless library."

"Shall we burn it down?" Navi asks, a hollow grin tugging at her lips. "The entire castle, so Maaz wins nothing."

I shake my jaguar head. "No, she would only dance over the rubble."

"Indeed." Navi's sword clanks as she shifts.

"Tell me, Navi," I say softly. "Should I have agreed to her terms?"

Navi snorts. "Absolutely not, Altair."

"Why?"

She turns her steely gaze towards me. "Because that witch would have destroyed this kingdom a thousand years ago, right after she laid claim to it. She would have razed it to the ground and her cruel Sisters would have run amok among our people. No, you did the right thing refusing her."

"And yet, here we are." I tilt my chin towards the city below. "Maaz will still burn it down. But she'll have no people to toy with."

"And that's a comfort," Navi mutters.

"In a way," I agree halfheartedly. "What time is it?"

"Half past seven," Navi says.

"Sixteen hours to go," I sigh. "How shall we spend it?"

Navi takes a deep breath and then drops to one knee. She bows her head in obeisance. "My King."

"Navi, what are you doing?" I say incredulously. She hasn't bent the knee for me in over a thousand years.

She doesn't look up. "My King, I have served you for one thousand, three hundred, and sixteen years. I have been loyal to my King and the Kingdom. I pledged my life to yours to die protecting you. But I would pledge my life to bind myself to you. My heart."

I go still as I realize just what she speaks of. A sacred binding. The kind I would ask Verity to make. And Verity alone. I sit up and flare my wings out behind me. "Navi, rise," I say.

"My King, I would ask that you respond first," she murmurs. "Tell me your answer."

"I cannot." I wish desperately that I wasn't this beast. I wish that I could show her how her words have touched me. She looks up, brows flat. "I can't return your feelings, Navi. I'm in love with another."

"You're in love with her," she says flatly.

"I am." I nod. "Please, get up."

In one swift motion, Navi is on her feet, her sword sheathed again. "Don't let this trouble you, Altair." Her lips tug upwards into a kind smile. "With only sixteen hours left in this world with you, I wanted you to know."

"Thank you, Navi," I whisper.

She bows and disappears down the stairs. I imagine I hear an echo of a stifled cry as her footsteps fade. I met Navi when we were young Fae; young and impulsive and wild. There was a time we turned to each other in our pain, but that was long ago. Navi's cold and stony demeanor almost convinced me that she would never love anyone. I was wrong.

Sorrow lances through my heart. I wish I could return her feelings. How easy that would be. But on the last day of my life, I don't want to deny how I feel any longer. Like Navi, I need to be honest with myself. And with Verity.

I turn away, studying the city again. My people know what's coming tonight. They know that time is up. Maaz will come tonight, while we are all faded away, and claim my kingdom for herself.

Fury sweeps through me as I picture Maaz in my mind. Her slender figure draped in a long, red cloak. She would tear it all down just to spite me, even after I'm gone. I should send Verity back through the portal before that moment comes. Sighing, I turn away from the view and slip over the rim of the tower. The wind rushes through the feathers of my wings and ruffles my short fur. I close my eyes, relishing the freedom of the free fall before spreading my wings wide.

I catch myself a few meters from the ground and soar upwards, back into the sky. I find Verity in the wild garden again, pacing agitatedly. She barely glances up as I land on the lawn beside her. "I don't understand," she mutters angrily.

I cock my head, watching her as she rubs at her temples. "What is it, Verity?"

"I have tried everything I can think of," she snaps. "I have brewed potions, cast spells, I even kissed you hoping it would reverse the curse. But nothing works! And I've read every damn book in that damn library about this damn magic!"

"Verity," I say, keeping my voice low and soothing.

"What?" She whirls on me.

I brush a wing over her, the closest I can come to stroking her in this form. "You'll have to return to the mortal realm tonight."

"Why?" Her brows crumple. "It isn't—is it?"

"Tonight, near midnight, Maaz wins," I say, nodding. "I'll send you through the portal before the curse takes me and my people. You'll be safe from Maaz in the human realm."

"No." Verity shakes her head. "Why didn't you tell me it was this soon?"

I meet her gaze. The once vibrant blue is the gloomy shade of a stormy sea. "I thought it was best that you didn't know."

"You can't decide what's best for me, Altair," she whispers.

"You're right. I'm sorry." I drop my head, fatigue and exhaustion weighing on me. Years of dreading this day, and now it's finally arrived. It's all very surreal.

"I wish we had more time," she breathes, her voice breaking.

I look up as she drops to her knees beside me. Her arms wrap around my neck and she nuzzles her face into my fur. I purr, closing my eyes. "Why?"

She shakes her head against me. "I didn't get my fill of your incessant teasing."

"Verity," I murmur. "Tell me, please. Why do you want more time?"

"I told you," she says into my fur. "I just didn't get enough of you."

"What more do you want?" I say as her arms tighten around me. "I will give you everything."

Verity pulls away, her eyes wide. She flushes slightly and bites her lip. "You don't mean that."

Before I can speak, she jumps to her feet and runs from the garden. My heart clenches painfully in my chest as her slim figure disappears around one of the hedges. "Everything," I say aloud, wishing she could hear me. "I will give you everything."

CHAPTER 20

Verity

Altair's words echo through my head as I run through the library. My fingers drift over countless spines, searching for any tome that could help me to break the curse. I will give you everything. My breath hitches in my throat, heart pounding wildly.

It wasn't like Altair. Sarcastic and mysterious, he wouldn't be so honest. Would he? My heart clenches as I remember the moment; the sincerity in his eyes. Those gorgeous hazel eyes. I scan text after text, hoping for anything to scream out at me. But there's nothing here. Nothing that I haven't read or checked already.

Frustration and despair sweep through me, like a roiling cloud. I toss a book to the ground with a shout, and then stand, panting, over it. His last day. His last day and he didn't tell me. If I had known, I would have spent every waking minute I had in this library, rather than at his side, flirting with him. How could I be so stupid? How could I have taken is so lightly?

I drop into a crouch and clutch at my head. It pounds steadily, painfully. But what can I do?

"Child," the librarian's wizened voice reaches me as the sun sets.

I glance up, surprise arching my brows. "I thought everyone had left."

"Everyone else," the librarian confirms, sweeping towards me. "But this library is my home."

"You live in here?" I ask, dropping my hands from my face.

"You look troubled," she says.

I heave a sigh. "Today is the last day, and I can't do anything to help Altair or the Fae. They're all going to die because of me."

"They'll die because of Maaz," she corrects, her tone light. "Listen to me now."

"Why?" I ask warily.

Her eyes flash. "The Bloodbane witches covenant with the Dark God, Sadal Melik. It is he who gives them their powers."

"Yes." I nod exasperatedly. "It's called the Blood Rite, they become his brides. And they never turn away. If they do, they die."

"Indeed. You, my little mortal, are a Bloodbane witch. But when did you make your covenant?" She cocks a brow.

"I didn't," I whisper. "I was born with it."

"Were you?" She asks, turning away.

I scramble to my feet, skin tingling. "What do you mean?"

"You don't expect me to reveal everything, do you?" The librarian flashes me a sly smile. "Good luck, dear."

I bite my lip, pondering her words. Maybe my magic doesn't work because I haven't made the covenant with Sadal Melik. I grimace. I don't know that I want to become the bride of an evil god from this dimension. But if it's the only way to save Altair, I would do it. I would give him everything.

There was a reason Altair brought me here, a reason that he needed a woman with the power to become a Bloodbane witch. But if he only needed the covenant, surely any Bloodbane would do. But they wouldn't help him, I realize. Any Bloodbane that helps a sworn enemy would lose their place in the Sisterhood at Maaz's command. Maybe even Sadal Melik's command.

I rush from the library as the castle is cast in darkness. There are no servants to light the candles and lamps that fill the halls. I run through the shadows to Altair's room. I burst in, stubbing my toe on the door. "Damn!" I shout, hissing in pain.

But the room is empty. His bed carefully made, and the fire burnt out. My heart lurches in my chest and my breath quickens. What if he's already been taken from me? What if I'm alone in the castle? Breathing shakily, I whirl away from his room and back through the halls. Every shadow and every object in the darkness looks like Maaz.

"Altair?" I shout, sprinting as I feel the darkness at my back. Fear sweeps through me, stabbing my heart like a lance. "Altair!"

But the castle is silent. My feet slap against the stone floor loudly as I jump from the stairs onto the landing. My eyes are rimmed with tears, my throat swollen with grief. I can hardly breathe, but I run on anyway. I have to find him. Altair. Altair. Altair.

A tear slips from my eyes and I wipe it away furiously. I have never felt more alone than I do now. An entire kingdom gone. And just me left to fill it. Suddenly, I see a light spilling out of an open door ahead. The door is tall and covered in carved wooden vines. I pause in front of it and peer through it. This door has been locked tightly since I first arrived in the castle.

The light is almost blinding compared to the darkness of the halls. But when my eyes adjust, I see a simple golden throne on a marble dais. And in it sits Altair. A sob slips from my parted lips and I cover my mouth with a shaky hand. His hazel eyes dart towards me, wide with worry. He rises and holds a hand out towards me.

"Verity?" His voice echoes through the grand hall.

"Altair," I whisper, rushing towards him.

I cover the distance in seconds, and he wraps his strong arms around me. "Verity, what's wrong?" His voice is laced with worry and fear.

"I thought you were gone," I whisper, trying to control my ragged breathing.

"No." He strokes my hair gently as I lean into his chest. "No, I wouldn't go without saying goodbye."

I push him away from me, my fear giving way to anger. "Don't do that to me!" I shout. "God, I- I was so scared, Altair."

"I'm sorry." His brows crumple.

Silence falls between us, hollow and loud in the massive room. I break my gaze with him and finally take in the space. Marble columns line the length of the room, the floor is inlaid with a detailed tile mosaic of a hawk. Altair perches on the armrest of the throne, watching me.

"What is this place?" I ask, my voice echoing through the room.

"My throne room," he says, gesturing grandly. "I haven't used it in years. This is where Maaz cursed me. I've kept it locked ever since. It seemed a fitting place to meet my end." I stare at him. "Parallelism and all that."

"Are you okay?" I ask softly, moving closer to him.

He reaches for me, trailing his fingers down my arm tenderly. And I remember his words. Everything. "I'm fine, Verity. But we should get you home soon."

"I know where the portal is." I clench my hands into fists, forcing the well of emotions back. "When it's done, I'll go. But I won't go before."

"You want to stay with me? Watch me waste away in a matter of seconds?" He cocks a brow. "Absolutely not."

I drop my voice to a whisper. "You can't decide what's best for me, Altair."

He chuckles. "In this case, I can, and I will."

"No," I say forcefully, crossing my arms.

"Verity," Altair growls. "Don't be stubborn. Please, just once, listen to me."

I eye him. "Where is Navi?"

"Navi is performing her last watch. That was her wish," Altair says stiffly.

I can picture her now, on the battlements, her sword in hand, standing proud and strong. "I wish I had gotten to know her better."

"Perhaps it's best that you didn't," Altair says as a smile tugs at his lips.

"Altair," I say. I grab his hand tightly in mine, my gut coiled with nerves. "I have to tell you something. Ask you something. I don't know."

"What is it?" His brows furrow with concern.

But before I can speak, the doors at the opposite end of the hall slam open. They smash loudly against the walls, the sound echoing through the throne room. Fear courses through me as Maaz saunters into the room. She has a broom in her hand, a slight thing of pale wood. When she sees us on the throne, she grins broadly; a smile so wide it looks like a crocodile grinning at me. I shudder as she tosses her broom aside and stops at the foot of the dais.

"Hello, darling," she says sweetly.

"Maaz," Altair growls. He pushes me behind him protectively.

Her eyes glitter. "I've come to collect."

"I'm afraid that you're several hours too early, Maaz," Altair snaps. "You grow so impatient just before the end. You've waited a thousand years, surely you can wait a few hours more."

Maaz taps her chin, feigning thoughtfulness. "You always made such excellent points, Altair. Really, but I simply don't see what another hour is to you. You're dead anyway."

"Not. Yet." Altair stands taller.

Maaz sighs dramatically and turns her cold eyes on me. "I saw you at the ball. Sniffed out your Bloodbane blood a mile away."

She tosses her blonde hair over her shoulder. "If I had wanted to, I could have cut you down that night."

I narrow my eyes at her. "Aren't I lucky."

Maaz laughs, tossing her head back. Suddenly, her laughter falls silent and she snaps her head back towards me. A chill curls down my spine. "You think you're funny. Do you know who I am?"

"Maaz," I say stiffly. "Leader of the Bloodbane."

"Of which you are one," she snaps.

"Not yet," I breathe.

She pauses, her head cocked to the side. "What did you say?"

"I am not a Bloodbane yet," I say, louder this time.

Maaz purses her lips and falls into a more relaxed stance. She picks at her nails. "It doesn't matter now, does it? You've already lost, Altair. And I've won."

Altair shakes his head as his hand reaches back to close over mine. "Not completely, Maaz." He grins. "My heart belongs to another. Even in death, you can never have it."

Maaz colors, her shoulders stiff. "As if I would want it, anymore. Now you're weak," she spits. "And I have no more time for you."

I narrow my eyes at her words, suspicion tickling my mind. But Maaz puts a hand on her hip, surveying us. Altair releases my hand and clenches his own into fists at his sides. I can feel the anger rolling off of him in waves. But Maaz seems unbothered. Her eyes glitter.

"Altair," I whisper as the realization hits me.

But it's too late, Maaz flings the dagger that was strapped to her back at Altair. The metal sings as it tumbles through the air, silver and blinding. I scream, the sound shattering the silence. I hear Altair inhale sharply as he realizes what Maaz has done. His last breath.

My mind is a wash of memories of Altair and fear. I feel his warm body beneath my hands, his muscles tense and hard. I stumble forward, moving into the space he once occupied. I feel the cold first, cold right in my gut, like an icicle. The pain follows the cold after a moment, intense and washing through my entire body.

I look down at the silver dagger protruding from my belly. It's so much smaller up close. I let out a ragged breath as I fall to my knees, the pain from the fall only secondary to the wound. I can hear Altair shouting beside me, but it feels so far away. Eyes wide, I search for him. He hovers over me, taking my shoulders in his arms as he lowers me to the ground.

Blood coats his hands as he tentatively touches the wound. I shake my head as stinging pain shoots through me. "Verity," he whispers, his voice finally reaching me. "Gods, Verity."

"Altair," I gasp.

His voice cracks. "Verity, why? Oh, Gods."

"How sad." Maaz pouts. "I was looking forward to bringing her into the fold."

"You," Altair whispers. His shoulders quake and his hazel eyes flash furiously. "I'll kill you. I will fucking kill you."

"Altair," I rasp. He turns back to me, his eyes filled with tears.

"Don't talk, I can fix this," Altair murmurs, lifting a trembling hand to my forehead.

I can feel my own blood smear across my forehead as he gently strokes me. "Altair, I know what to do," I breathe. The pain is almost overwhelming. "I know how to save you."

"Hush," he says gently. "It's over now. You don't have to try anymore."

"No." I shake my head, wincing. "I, Verity Chastain, bind my life to yours. I will give you all of me. I will make my vows to you instead of the Dark God."

As I say the words that have echoed through my mind since the librarian disappeared, I can feel my blood singing through my veins. Altair's eyes widen, his lips parted in surprise. I offer him a smile, but I know it looks more like a grimace. From the dais, I can see Maaz's face go pale, and I know that I've won.

I wheeze as more blood pours from the wound, drenching my tunic and spilling over the marble floor. "Did it work?"

Altair presses his lips to my bloodied forehead. "It will. For I will bind myself to you, Verity Chastain. I accept your covenant."

As he says the words, a gust of wind bursts from the dais, breezing powerfully through the throne room and beyond. I sigh and fall back to the marble floor, eyes heavy with fatigue. I've done it. We've done it. Happiness swells in my chest for a single instant before I remember suddenly that death is near.

"How dare you?" Maaz shrieks. "It doesn't matter if she's broken the curse. I'll still kill you and claim what's mine."

Altair rises slowly to his feet, his expression cold and cruel. A shiver slips through me at the sight. He turns to Maaz, flexing his hands. "It isn't yours."

CHAPTER 21

Altair

Verity's blood coats my hands and stains my leather boots. She's bleeding out quickly and will die soon if I can't help her. The dagger still juts from her gut, but I know removing it will only make things worse. Her eyes are half-closed as she takes short and shallow breaths. The joy I felt when she swore to bind herself to me lasted only an instant before my rage towards Maaz pushed it aside. There will be time to celebrate later.

"My soldiers are coming," I murmur. "They will have felt the curse lift."

I turn to Maaz, my eyes blazing with fury. She sweeps her cloak back, exposing more daggers sheathed at her waist, though I know she'll use her magic against me as well. Her beautiful face is twisted into a gruesome grimace, her slender figure trembling.

"Get out, Maaz," I snarl. "Before I rip you apart with my bare hands and feed you to my hounds."

"Never," she sneers. "I've waited a thousand years for this."

I step down from the dais slowly, my footsteps echoing in the massive, empty chamber. "Good. Now I can savor killing you."

With a scream, she slings another silver dagger towards me.

But I'm ready now. Quick as a cat, I snatch the blade from mid-air and toss it between my hands, chuckling softly. "I feel better than I have in years, Maaz. Stronger. Faster."

"Cruento," Maaz hisses, her fingers splayed towards me.

Thin, needle-like mirrors streak towards me, whistling through the air. I dart to the side, ducking just as one of the magical blade's glides over my head. I right myself and turn towards Maaz, but she's disappeared. The skin on the back of my neck tingles. I whirl around just as she swings a dagger at my throat, narrowly missing puncturing my jugular.

I lunge towards her, blade twisting in my hand as I slash at her. She jumps back, her cloak and heavy skirts rustling. With a snarl, she thrusts the long dagger towards my gut. I roll to the side, sweeping my blade out to nick her in the ribs. She gasps sharply, glowering. I prowl around her as she touches a finger to the wound, bleeding lightly. Blood coats her pale finger and I grin. Maaz lifts her finger to her lips, her tongue darting out to lick the blood from her skin.

My brows furrow with disgust as she smiles cruelly. "Sicaòr," she whispers.

A gust of wind blows through the throne room, it carries a sickly-sweet stench. When the breeze brushes my cheeks, I feel a stinging pain as it peels the skin from my face, layer by layer. Hissing, I dart towards her, blade angled for her chest. She spins away, laughing. But I anticipated this. I tangle my fingers through her hair, dragging her backwards.

Maaz cries out as I tear at her hair. She struggles against me, ripping bits of her scalp. Blood stains her roots as she releases a shrill scream. I yank her towards me, my blade poised to fall over her exposed chest.

"I will relish killing you," I murmur, eyes glimmering.

My blade plummets towards her. In a blur of motion, her hand rises to fend off the blow and with a sickening squelch, the blade slips through her palm. She snarls and my eyes widen as she forces her palm upwards, forcing the dagger through completely. Maaz pushes me back, her slender arms surprisingly strong.

Blood drains from the wound, streams of it coating her wrist and running down her forearms. Scowling, I wrench the dagger free of her palm, blood arcing through the air. I whirl as she cradles her wounded palm to her chest. Her pale blue eyes narrow coldly.

"I'll remember this," she growls.

I twirl the blade in my hand, spinning it between my fingers. "You won't remember anything."

Without warning, I fling the dagger towards her, straight between her eyes. Maaz raises her injured hand, her bloodied palm facing me. Wordlessly, she stops the dagger in mid-air. I glower as she shatters the blade into tiny, dust-sized fragments.

She smirks, her eyes following the particles as they float away. I'm on top of her before she knows it, my shoulders slamming into her chest. She topples backwards onto her back. I straddle her waist, my hands wrapping around her slim throat. I can feel her blood pulsing beneath my grip. She takes a ragged breath and claws at my face, her nails drawing blood.

I growl, squeezing tighter. Maaz's face goes blue, her eyes bulging. A drop of my blood trickles from my chin and splatters on her cheek, stark against the pale porcelain of her skin. She trembles, her clawing growing weaker and weaker. I grin ferally, eyes gleaming.

Suddenly, I'm blown backwards by a violent burst of energy. I somersault through the air, knees bouncing painfully off the floor. Swiftly, I roll into a crouch, fists bared for an attack. Maaz clambers to her feet, a hand at her throat. She wheezes, her shoulder shaking. She's spent, I realize with a smirk.

"This isn't over," she rasps, a hand on her deadwood broom. "It's far from over. Your day of reckoning will come."

Before I can respond or leap to my feet to chase her, she's

mounted her broom and launched herself through one of the stained-glass windows in the throne room. Glass shatters, tinkling like bells as it strikes the marble floor. All that's left of Maaz is her blood pooling on the floor. I pant, staring at the shattered window.

"Altair," Verity whispers behind me.

My blood runs cold as I pivot and sprint towards her. I cover the distance in two long strides, skidding to my knees beside her. She's paler than before, as white as paper. Even her rosy lips have lost their color. I grind my teeth, finding her hand blindly and clutching it. She squeezes my hand, so lightly I hardly feel it.

"The healers are coming," I murmur, brushing her light brown hair back.

"It's too late," she says softly, pinching her face.

"Not for us." I force a reassuring smile. "I'm taking the dagger out. It will hurt."

She chuckles breathlessly. "I don't feel anything anymore."

"Good." I nod.

I pray that she forgives me. Without warning, I wrench the silver blade from her belly, blood spurting from the wound. She cries out sharply, her face twisted in pain. I drop the blade and press my hands to the wound. Her warm blood slips through my fingers.

I hear shouting in the distance, my soldiers returning from Desmarais. The door slams open and Navi runs through, her eyes wide. I turn to her and grimace. "She's dying," I say, voice cracking.

Navi's eyes dart around the room, taking in the scene, before she closes the distance between us. She tears off the sash at her waist and shoves me aside. Her sash is soon wet with blood, but the flow seems to be ebbing. Whether from her efforts or because Verity is almost dead, I don't know.

"Soldiers were right behind me, there will be healers among them," she says confidently.

The chattering grows louder, followed by thumping footsteps. In an instant, the throne room is flooded with soldiers. One of them kneels beside us, studying Verity's wounds. I watch, breath coming in short gasps, as he lifts the sash.

"Can she be saved?" I ask. My fingers wrap around Verity's ankle. I need to touch her, to feel her.

"Perhaps," he murmurs. "You must go, I need more healers."

"I won't," I snap. "I stay with her."

The healer turns his brown eyes to me. "Go, my King."

"How dare you," I hiss, leaning towards him threateningly.

Navi's hand closes around my arm and she drags me to my feet. I slap her hand away, trembling. She looks at me with disinterest. "Let the healers work. You won't help if you hover over her."

I inhale sharply, trying to control my breathing. "I know. I know," I say shakily. I turn to the healer. "Do whatever you must. Anything."

He nods seriously and then focuses on Verity as a cluster of healers join him. I glance back once more as Navi leads me from the dais. Verity is unconscious, her chest rising and falling shallowly. I pray to the gods for the first time in a thousand years. I pray that Verity will live.

Navi ushers me towards the broken window. "What happened here?" She asks, hand on the hilt of her sword.

"Maaz came to collect early," I say stiffly, staring towards the healers gathered around Verity's prone form. "When Verity broke the curse, she attacked me. Verity pushed me aside. I tried to stop her, but she escaped."

Navi looses a long breath. "I'm sorry I wasn't here. I failed in my duty."

"Nonsense," I murmur. "We each prepared ourselves differently for the end. I don't fault you for that."

"And the curse is broken," Navi says softly, following my gaze towards Verity. "How did she do it?"

"Just as Maaz required. She offered to bind herself to me, to covenant with me instead of Sadal Melik. She will never be his bride." I press my lips into a thin line. "Though I'm not entirely sure she knew what she was doing."

Navi peers up at the shattered window. "There will be time to explain when she's recovered. When the kingdom recovers."

"I want all the border patrols strengthened, men stationed at every tower," I say.

"Of course, Altair." Navi dips her chin sharply.

I meet her emerald gaze. "Maaz will be back. She's lived for an eternity, a small hiccup in her plans won't drive her away for long."

"And we'll be ready for her," Navi says firmly. "This time."

"I pray we are," I whisper.

I watch, eyes sorrowful, as the healers maneuver Verity onto a stretcher and lift her gently. Her soft groan echoes through the throne room and my brows furrow at the sound. Pain lances through my heart as I picture the moment she saved me from Maaz's blade. It's my fault she was so close to death. Guilt mingles with sorrow, coiling like ice in my heart. She disappears from view as the healers carry her into the hallway.

I turn back to the window. Maaz's blood stains the remaining shards. A wild and dangerous grin splits my lips. Maaz won't be long for this world. Not when I've been restored to my power and have every motive for revenge.

Maaz will feel my wrath soon.

And I'll make sure that it will hurt.

ALSO BY BAILEY DARK

Mated to The Fae King

(Completed Series - Fantasy Romance)

Also Available in Audio!

1. Stolen by The Fae King

2. Destined for The Fae King

3. Seduced by The Fae King

4. Claimed by The Fae King

5. Forever with The Fae King

Captive of Shadows

(Completed Series - Fantasy Romance)

Also Available in Audio!

1. Promised to The Shadow King

2. Trial for The Shadow King

3. Awakened by The Shadow King

4. Battle for The Shadow King

5. Eternity with The Shadow King

Warlords of Farian

(Completed Series - SciFi Romance)

1. The Beast King's Bride

2. Taken by The Alpha Warlord

3. The Commander's Virgin Queen

4. The Barbarian's Captive

5. Chosen by The Berserker

Warlords of Farian The Complete Boxed Set

Moon Cursed

(Current Series - Paranormal Romance)

Also Available in Audio!

1. Her Shifter King

2. Her Shifter Mate

3 -TBA

The Labyrinth Curse

(Current Series - Fantasy Romance)

Coming Soon in Audio!

1. The Twisted King

2. Coming Soon!

3. TBA

Destined for The Fae King
(Mated to The Fae King - Book Two)

"She shivers as I drag my tongue across her jugular. It's been too long since I kissed this woman. Too long since I felt her heat in my arms. She writhes against me, panting, and I grin ferally. "

Verity Chastain almost died saving her sadistic, charming kidnapper from the curse that threatened to take his life and destroy his kingdom. But something awoke inside her when she broke his curse, something dark.

Struggling to discover her past and her future, Verity pulls away from the one man who could save her. With their relationship fraying at the seams, Altair is desperate to find a way to save his kingdom from the Bloodbane witches. When news arrives that the Bloodbane are preparing to start a war, Altair's desperation reaches new heights.

Dark forces are brewing on Alnembra's borders, as they are in Verity's heart.

Chapter One

Verity

The healer bends over my belly, his lips pursed as they study what's left of the stab wound. I wince as he prods the laceration delicately; even the smallest touches send the pain flaring. He murmurs to himself and then withdraws a salve from his robes. It smells pungent, like ginger or mustard. I wrinkle my nose as he swipes the yellow cream over the gash in my belly.

Almost every day the healers have a new cream to apply to aid in the healing process. They seem almost baffled that I haven't healed completely yet after two weeks. But I'm human, not Fae. I clamber to my feet and lift my arms so the healer can wrap a bandage around my belly. His fingers are cool and nimble, like little kisses of snow against my skin.

When he's finished, I tug my shirt back down over my belly. He passes me the cane with a smile. "Many blessings, Curse-Breaker," he says bowing.

I force a smile. "Many blessings."

Curse-Breaker. That's what the servants and healers have been calling me in whispered breaths. No one saw what happened between Altair, Maaz, and I. No one knows that breaking the curse was as simple as pledging my life to his – whatever that means. I inhale sharply, staring into empty space. I know what it means. I know what it meant.

I swallow thickly. My engagement to Henry ended in such a mess I'm in no hurry to be engaged again. And yet here I am – sworn to a Fae King. The cane is a heavy weight in my hands as I force myself to lean on it and leave the healer's chambers. I do my best to stand tall while supporting myself on the cane, but in the end, I look like a hunched old woman.

I pass halls filled with smiling servants and stoic guards. They bow or curtsy as I pass before returning to their duties. I don't think I'll ever get used to the strange obeisance they show me. I'm not a Curse-Breaker or a hero, I'm just a girl. Altair hasn't noticed any difference in the Fae's behavior, but he's kept busy running his country for the first time in a thousand years.

I bite my lip as I think of him; the man I swore myself to. He hasn't pressed me for marriage yet, but I can only assume that's because of my injury. I almost don't want the gash to heal if it can put off my future. My uncertain future. With the wound, I know what happens day in and day out.

Breakfast. Reading. Lunch. Healers. Dinner. A short visit from Altair. Sleep.

The days are boring and drag on, but I know at the end of them I won't be pressed for decisions. There's too much for me to think about. Too many questions. And right now, the only question on my mind, the only one that constantly plagues me, is who I am. What I am. I slow as I approach the library. The halls are always emptier around the library, I don't feel so rushed to make my way out of the eyes of the servants and guards.

Altair and others insist that the Bloodbane oath flows through my veins. I know it's true. I felt it when the witches kidnapped me and held me so tightly. I felt it when I said the words that ended Altair's curse. I feel it now. My Bloodbane ancestry is like lead in my veins. I feel it always, a constant pressure. It's a reminder of what abilities and powers lie in store for me. Even that is a mystery. Altair refuses my questions about the Bloodbane, my requests to know my own history. I grimace, my past and future feels lost to me.

At the door of the library I pause and catch my breath. Walking long distances, even from one end of the palace to the other, often leaves me short of breath now. I come to the library almost every day searching for answers or clues as to who I am and what my covenant with Altair means.

This world of magic, Fae, and witches is new to me. New and unfamiliar. And wholly different from anything I expected when I imagined these fantastical realms before. There is only one thing about myself and my blood I'm certain of. The Bloodbane witches gain their power from their binding to Sadal Malik. They wed him figuratively and he gives them their power. He would have given me my power if I had said my oath to him and not Altair.

I don't know what happens to me now that I'll be binding myself to another man and not the Dark God. Another question no one has been able to answer. Perhaps I won't have access to powerful magic anymore. Maybe nothing will change at all. After all, Altair isn't an ancient god. But ever since I said the words, the oath in my veins has been singing constantly. Waiting for something. Or someone.

I shake my head, trying to clear my mind of the anxiety I feel almost constantly now. I head to the far corner of the library, where the tomes on magic and the Bloodbane witches are kept. With the cane in one hand, and two heavy texts in the other, I waddle back to the center of the room to a chair pushed up beside the window.

With a grunt, I heave the books onto an adjacent table and

settle carefully into the chair. Sunshine pours through the windows, warming my chilled skin. I open the first book and flip to the first page. It's a history of the Bloodbane witch clans. There are five in total, with many divisions within the major clans. They have a complex structure of leadership. But their Chieftess is always the strongest among them. Maaz.

I feel a tingle of fear trickle down my spine as I think of her. She's ancient; several thousand years old. And she's led the Bloodbane witches for most of them. I remember her cruel, blue eyes as she glowered at me during our last encounter. She was murderous and frightening. The memory of her blade burying itself in my belly after she threw it towards Altair sends my heart racing. I'm breathing too quickly, too shallowly. I clutch the arm rests beside me, digging my nails into the soft velvet.

Panic floods through me and it's as if I'm back in that moment when I thought my life was ending. The pain in my belly flares as my blood pumps faster. I know it's slipping through the stitches now and beginning to soak the bandage. I clench my eyes shut, forcing myself to take deep breaths.

I lurch as I feel a strong hand on my shoulder. "It's okay, Verity, you're safe," Altair murmurs.

My eyes open enough to see him crouch in front of me. He presses his hands on my legs, attempting to ground me. "Altair," I whisper fearfully.

"Shh." His brows are furrowed. "Breathe."

After a few moments of struggling to catch my breath, I feel my heart settle. I inhale deeply and then release the breath slowly. My muscles relax, and I can finally open my eyes completely. "I'm sorry," I say as I stare into his hazel eyes.

His black hair is swept back, revealing the tips of his pointed ears. His full lips are pulled into a concerned smile. My eyes rake over his frame. Even crouched before me, it's obvious that he's tall and lean. His tunic is unlaced near the collar, just enough to reveal a slip of hair.

"You have nothing to be sorry for," he says. I nod. Altair takes the book from my lap and inspects it. "Just a bit of light reading?"

I blanch, knowing what he thinks of me learning about the Bloodbane. "I know it's dangerous to involve myself with Bloodbane magic, but it's part of who I am. And since the curse was broken, I've felt so lost," I say softly.

"What do you mean?" He frowns.

I bite my lip. "Whether you or I like it, I am a Bloodbane. At least, almost. But now that I've made my vow to you and not to Sadal Melik, I don't know what happens next. I don't know what happens to me and my magic."

"It's a little early in your life to be having an existential crisis," he says, cocking a brow.

"Altair." I glower at him.

He laughs softly. "I know." His eyes grow serious and his voice lowers. "You're Verity Chastain, you're the Curse-Breaker. And my future wife."

My heart beats wildly at his words. Curse-Breaker. Wife. "That's a lot to put on a librarian's shoulders," I whisper. My gut is twisted and heavy.

"You've been cooped up in this castle for too long," Altair quips, rising. "Let me take you to see Desmarais, the City of Glass."

I furrow my brows and sink back into the chair. "Is it safe?"

"You don't have to worry, Verity," Altair says gently. "Maaz and her witches are far from Desmarais."

"I can hardly walk." I tilt my chin towards the cane next to me. "I barely made it from the healer's tower to the library."

"Not to worry; I'll take you on a grand tour in my carriage," Altair says.

I purse my lips but rise shakily to my feet. I am eager to get out of the palace and the palace grounds. The palace is all I've seen of Altair's kingdom, except the wilderness from my last abduction. I reach for my cane, grimacing in pain, but excitement tugs at my heart. I feel lighter already.

"Is it really that terrible?" He asks, cocking a brow.

"I feel like an old woman," I sigh.

Suddenly, Altair's strong arms sweep me off my feet. He lifts me into the air easily and holds me against his chest. My eyes widen and I gasp softly at the sudden move. My cane clatters to the floor, the sound echoing through the empty library. Altair's eyes rove over me, a smile playing at his lips. An image of the two of us pressed together, lips trailing kisses over bare skin, flits through my mind. My cheeks heat at the thought, but I can't tear my gaze away from his full lips.

"I can walk on my own," I say, wiggling in his arms.

A soft purr rumbles from his chest. "I can't let a woman as beautiful as you suffer."

"Altair," I say, my voice carrying a hint of a whine.

"Do you want me to drop you?" He cocks a brow.

I yelp as he relaxes his arms long enough to let me slip a few inches closer to the ground. "You are such a bastard," I hiss, clinging to his chest.

Altair chuckles low, adjusting his grip. His hand grazes my ass and my breath hitches in my throat. "If that's what I have to be for the pleasure of feeling you in my arms," he purrs. I go stiff, a blush creeping to my cheeks. "Do you know it's been weeks since I last held you close?"

"No," I stammer. I've kept Altair at a distance since the night I broke his curse.

"Liar," he murmurs. "Let me hold you like this."

We fall silent as he strides out of the library. I relax into his arms as he sweeps out the main door and down the castle steps to the awaiting carriage. I bite my lip as he sets me down gently in front of the door. I climb onto the first step, hands on the door frame to hoist myself in. I can feel Altair's eyes on me and it sends a thrill coursing through me.

There's a loud clatter and I turn instinctively to find the source of the noise. My heart beats out of time in my chest as I make eye contact with a Fae gardener. His eyes are a deep brown, black from a distance, and his skin is pale like ivory. He's tall, with a lithe figure. His lips are quirked into a wicked smile as I meet his gaze. He turns away to pick up his fallen tools and I can't help but stare at his lean muscles. It feels as if time itself has frozen in that instant, everything falls away except the gardener's eyes.

Behind me, Altair gently nudges one of my hands free, as if to assist me. I blink, drawing my gaze away from the beautiful Fae. With Altair's help, I clamber into the carriage and settle in the corner. The cushions of the carriage seats are a plush, red velvet with gold trim. He slams the door as he sits. The carriage is large enough to fit Altair's large frame and then some.

We trundle away from the palace as I quell the excitement in my chest. Altair smiles at me from across the carriage; a patient, hopeful smile. I meet his gaze, chewing on my bottom lip. I'm not used to the thoughtful and kind version of Altair that he's projecting today. I turn away, pretending to stare at the palace grounds as we approach the gates. I imagine I see the gardener again, this time in the shade of a mulberry tree. I drag my gaze away from the tricky shadows and peek at Altair from behind a sheet of my brown hair.

He seems so at relaxed now that the curse is broken, and his country is his again. He's fallen back into his duties without any trouble, and I know it makes him happy to be working again. Be stagnant for so long should have driven him mad. He lounges back in the chair, comfortable in the silence between us. I should be happy for him. But my own questions and doubts are always lingering in the back of my mind, like a cobweb in the corner.

Chapter Two

Altair

Verity is warm in my arms as I carry through the castle halls. Her petite frame has grown even lighter in the past weeks since she's been injured. I hide a frown, wondering if she's eating well enough. I should be eating with her and spending more time with her, but my duties as King keep me away for most hours of the day.

I hold her a little closer, wishing again that she hadn't jumped in front of the blade for me. It shocked me then, and I still haven't been able to fully understand why she did it. Verity and I keep each other at arm's length despite what we've been through together. The only thing that brings me hope that she might feel as strongly for me as I do for her is that she sacrificed herself for me. She's settled in my arms, but her lips are twisted into an expression of discomfort. I suppose after losing so much precious time to be with her, it's only natural that we've lost the familiarity between us.

I don't know that I would even kiss her the way I used to. My heart clenches in my chest. Verity is to be my wife. I can't let this distance continue. It's too much already, a small rift between us where we should only be knitted closer together. She peeks up at me with her pale blue eyes and I grin at her. I'll pretend I'm not worried. I'll pretend that we're alright.

Outside, the sun is still high in the sky. It warms my skin and I smile more broadly. Only a few weeks ago, I hadn't felt the sun on my bare skin in a thousand years. I missed its warm glow. No one could possibly understand just how much I cherish being in my Fae form in broad daylight now. It's a gift.

The carriage is waiting outside and I set Verity in front of it gently. She pauses and stares into the distance, her hands on the doorframe. I trail a finger down her back and follow her gaze. There's a gardener collecting some fallen tools. He and Verity lock eyes before he glances sharply at me. I curl my lip at him on reflex, my more territorial Fae nature revealing itself. I nudge Verity forward, drawing her attention away from the handsome gardener. She moves sluggishly, as if waking from a dream.

I follow her into the carriage and draw the curtains on my side so the gardener is hidden from view. But Verity seems to have forgotten about him now; she stares out her own window at the familiar gardens.

I watch her carefully as she gazes out the window. The carriage rolls forward, following the long drive to the castle walls. She shrinks back into the cushions, covering her face with her long brown hair. I smile, pleased that Verity and I can finally enjoy time together. For the past two weeks, after the healers determined that she wasn't going to die, I've only been able to find a few minutes to spend with her. I drop my gaze as guilt tugs at my heart. I should find more time to spend with her.

She clears her throat. "Don't you have more to do as King?"

"I cancelled all of my appointments today," I explain, sliding across the bench so I'm directly across from her.

"Can you do that?" She looks surprised.

I place a hand on her knee and squeeze lightly. "The country was stagnant for a thousand years; it can be stagnant for another day."

Verity blushes softly and falls silent as we pass through the castle gates. The road to Desmarais is a decline, lined with tall trees and lamplights. There are a few wagons trundling down the road, returning from bringing goods to the castle. Verity leans forward, her face halfway out the window so she can take it all in. I feel a pang of regret that this is the first time verity has been out of the castle walls with permission. She was trapped like a little bird for so long. But there was no helping it; the Bloodbane witches would have killed her otherwise.

The wagons pull off the road to allow us to pass, they recognize the royal sigil on the doors. The castle slowly disappears above us, perched on a cliff that overlooks the city. Verity peers up at it, taking in the buttresses and elegant towers.

"Verity," I say softly as the scent of delicate spices reaches my nose. She turns at the sound of my voice and her eyes widen as she notices the sight laid out before her. "Welcome to Desmarais, the City of Glass."

Her lips are parted softly as we enter the outskirts of the city. The City of Glass is not named so because of its architecture or building materials, but rather because of the bright and pearlescent light that shines in the night and day. It glows merrily with lamplight that reflects off of the white stucco of the buildings. Verity's hands clutch the windowsill as she stares at the crowds of Fae wandering through the shopping streets. The road is lined with buildings packed side by side with large windows displaying baked goods, jewels, clothes, and more. Fae children dart between the carriages that wander down the road. She gasps at the sight of them and points.

I laugh. "Yes, there are children."

"How old?" She asks, her voice breathless with delight.

I peek out the window and squint at the children. "I would guess maybe seventy-five years old."

"Seventy-five," she echoes. She bursts into bright laughter and my heart warms at the sound. "They're older than me."

"It's been a long time since I heard you laugh," I murmur.

She glances at me, startled, and then bites her lip. "It's been a long time since I've laughed at all."

Wordlessly, I move across the carriage to sit beside her. She edges closer to the wall, away from me, pain lances through my chest but I try to ignore the subtle distance. I lean over her and point out the window, showing her the different sights of Desmarais.

"What's that?" Verity asks, pointing to a tall, white spire in the distance.

"That's the Library of Desmarais," I say. "It has the greatest collection of knowledge in the world."

"I thought your private library was impressive," she whistles softly. "I'd love to see it."

I smile. A visit to the library would be perfect for Verity. "Perhaps another day, they aren't open to the public. Even I have to arrange a visit beforehand."

"But you're the King," she says incredulously.

"Yes, but they're the librarians." I grin, nudging her shoulder gently. I peek out the window in time to see the window display of a famous jeweler in Desmarais. "Driver, stop here please."

The carriage rolls to a stop and Verity looks around, worry bunching her brows. "What are you doing?"

"I wanted to visit one of my favorite stores," I say, opening the door and crawling around her. I hop out of the carriage and onto the cobblestones. Verity bites her lip but takes my outstretched hand to leave the carriage.

"Is it alright for you to walk around like this? Out in the open?" She asks softly as the crowds of Fae go quiet.

They stare as we stride past. I lean close to her ear and when I speak, she shivers pleasantly. "Fae don't bite. Except on occasion," I tease her.

She purses her lips, glaring at me for a moment before suddenly lurching to the side. Panic flares in my belly as Verity presses herself into me, a soft whimper escaping her lips. I turn furious eyes on the Fae who startled her. But it's only an elderly Fae woman draped in a light shawl. I resist the urge to bare my teeth and, instead, only throw a protective arm around Verity.

"I'm sorry, Your Grace," the woman says in a lilting voice. "I didn't mean to startle her. I only wanted to thank the Curse-Breaker."

Verity stiffens at the name. I run my thumb over her arm to soothe her. "Lady Chastain," I say to the Fae. "You may call her Lady Chastain."

"Lady Chastain, you have my gratitude." The woman's voice trembles.

Verity nods. "It was nothing," she stammers.

Without another word, I lead Verity away from the Fae woman. Slowly, the Fae turn their attention away from us, having gotten their fill of the King and his Curse-Breaker. Verity detaches herself from me, wincing as pain lances through her belly. I glance back at the carriage, where her cane is tucked away.

"I'll get your cane," I say, turning away partially.

She latches onto my arm. "No," she says firmly. "I'm fine."

"Verity," I murmur.

"Show me the store, I want to see." She turns away from the carriage stubbornly.

I take her arm and show her to a jeweler renowned for his detail and artistry. The white of Desmarais is practically glowing under the sun. The glass windows of the shop glitter brilliantly as the sun strikes the jewels on display.

She blanches nervously at the decadent jewelry in the windows, but I push through the blue door and bring her into the elegant shop. The jeweler, a Fae man named Tinle, scurries from the back. His eyes widen as he takes me in. I extend a hand to him, grinning.

"Tinle, it's been a long time," I say warmly.

He bows before accepting my outstretched hand. "Your Grace, you do me a great honor."

"Tinle, I'd like you to meet Verity Chastain. Verity, this is the world's greatest jewel artist," I say.

Tinle scoffs in forced humility but doesn't deny my words. Verity dips her chin. "It's a pleasure to meet you."

"And you," Tinle says, his keen eyes roving over her. "What can I do for you, Your Grace?"

"I'm looking for something unique, something one of a kind for Verity," I say, following him to one of his display cases.

Tinle nods understandingly and disappears into the back. Verity tugs at my sleeve. "What are you doing?" She hisses under her breath.

"Buying you a gift." I smile, knowing that she'll only continue to protest.

"You don't have to," she says, a strain to her voice.

"I want to," I say firmly. I meet her gaze and squeeze her hand. "Let me, it's for my own benefit really. You would be doing me a favor."

She purses her lips. "Alright, but nothing too expensive."

"Verity," I murmur, leaning closer to her. "I have a thousand years of unspent gold, a thousand years of savings. I could buy you the world."

She gapes as Tinle returns, carrying a small silver box. He lays it gently on the display case and opens it with reverence. My lips part as I take in the delicate silver chain, studded with precious gems the color of my eyes.

Tinle grins, obviously pleased at my reaction. "It's amber," he says proudly.

"Fossilized tree sap?" Verity cocks a brow.

Tinle bristles. "Not just any amber. These particular stones were cut from amber found along the banks of the elusive Motabilem River."

I loose a breath, impressed. "And how were they acquired?"

"By an agent of mine many centuries ago. I've kept them locked up tight until the right buyer came along," Tinle explains.

"I don't understand." Verity glances between the two of us. "Why does this river make the amber more precious?"

"It's a moving river," I say.

"All rivers move," she says pointedly.

I chuckle. "No, the river is never in the same place. One day it could be deep in the mountains beyond our border, and the next, it could be south, pouring into the Azul sea. It might spend weeks in the Nubes Forest and then two days in Meridianam."

Her brows furrow. "How is it possible?"

I shrug. "No one knows."

Tinle straightens his shoulders. "As you can see, the gems are very precious."

"But how do we know they truly are from the Mo-," she trails off and then purses her lips. "This river?"

"Verity," I murmur. "Tinle is a man of great integrity."

Tinle lifts the necklace and hands Verity a delicate magnifying glass. "Look at the gem." He waits for her to peer at the stone. "Do you see the swirls of white in the gem? It's subtle, difficult to see."

"I see it," Verity says.

"The Motabilem River is unique in that its waters carry a strange liquid, which we can only assume is related to the magical way the river appears wherever it likes." Tinle drapes the necklace back in the box. "The presence of that material in the amber itself is an indication that it was taken from the banks of the Motabilem River."

Verity bites her lip. "I see. I meant no offense."

"It's alright," Tinle says. "You're mortal. You couldn't have known."

Verity's hands clench into fists at her sides, out of sight of Tinle. "Yes, I am mortal."

I slip my fingers into her clenched fists, forcing her hand to relax. "It's perfect, Tinle. I'll take it."

Tinle beams and rattles off a price. "Thank you, Your Grace." He bows as I pass him a purse of gold coin.

With Verity's hand in mine, we duck back out into the street, the silver box safely tucked in my pocket. I help her back into the carriage, noticing the way she visibly relaxes when she's finally out of sight of the Fae in the streets. Night is falling; the roads will soon be filled with Fae celebrations that last long into the night. I smirk, picturing the wild parties that stretch into the early dawn. Verity isn't quite ready for that yet. I eye her as she peers out the window. Maybe someday, but it will have to be a slow introduction.

As the carriage moves on, I settle next to Verity. I put the box in my lap and turn to her. "Turn around," I murmur.

She does as I say, peeking over her shoulder. I brush her hair away gently, my fingers grazing over her lovely porcelain skin. She shudders as I trail my touch over the sharp bones in her neck. If things were different between us, I might press my lips to the back of her neck in a soft kiss. But I won't press her; not when things are so delicate between us.

I drape the necklace over her head until it's settled against her chest. I clasp it, securing it around her neck. Reluctantly, I drop my hands away from her neck and back into my lap. She settles back against the seat and stares down at the necklace on her breast. She runs her hands over the amber stones.

"The color is the same as your eyes," she says softly.

"Is it?" I feign ignorance. "I hardly noticed."

She looks at me suspiciously but then her lips quirk into a smile. "I had no idea this world was so vast and diverse."

"Well, you've only seen a very small corner of it. My kingdom is small in comparison to others as well," I explain. "There's so much to see."

Verity fingers one of the gems. "I'd like to see this river someday."

"Perhaps I can take you," I say, hope swelling in my chest. This is what we need. We need more than my curse to build a relationship on. A thirst for adventure will do. I imagine Verity by my side as we take on the world and grin to myself. She's the only one I would want beside me.

"If you have time," she murmurs. "Being King has kept you busy."

I press my lips together in a thin line. "I'm sorry, Verity."

She falls silent and closes her eyes, as if she's tired. I wait for her to speak, but her lips never part. I leave her and drop my head back against the seat. I will do anything in my power to bring back a smile to Verity's face. I will chase her demons over the ends of the earth to bring her joy again. Something is eating at her, and I need to find out what.

Want to keep reading?
Grab Your Copy Now!

ABOUT THE AUTHOR

Bailey Dark is obsessed with all things dark, hot, and supernatural. From Fae to Aliens, her heroes are thoroughly alpha and pure raw masculinity. When she's not writing (which is hardly ever) she's busy watching every movie in the marvel universe, or binging supernatural on her couch. So come along, and enter her dark world. . . .

baileydarkauthor.com